SEARCHLIGHT

by Sara Fay

Society of Young Inklings

SOCIETY OF YOUNG INKLINGS

Searchlight
Copyright © 2015 Sara Fay

Requests for information should be addressed to:
Society of Young Inklings. PO Box 26914, San Jose, CA 95159

Editor: Ann Jacobus
Copyeditor: Sarah Rogers
Cover Design: Cindy Derby
Interior Design and Composition: Naomi Kinsman

Printed in the USA
First Printing: June 2015
ISBN 978-0-9910031-4-3

To my parents, Flo, Ansley, Tris, Lauren,
and my favorite consulting Brit.

"There is nothing to writing. All you do is sit down at a typewriter and bleed."
- Ernest Hemingway

"If I do not write to empty my mind, I go mad."
- Lord Byron

"I'm sending out my searchlight
Keep it on until I find you
You can bring me back to life
Because my heart's in smithereens
I need to feel what it's like
To be encompassed by you, oh
So I'm sending out my searchlight
To lead you back to me"

- Thomas Matthew, "Searchlight"

CONTENTS

CHAPTER ONE
YOUR NARRATOR

I've watched lots of people, I've seen lots of lives play out, and I've been a part of millions upon millions of lives. People seek me out. They use me in expressions, and I'm what half of the world is looking for as the other half runs away.

Who am I?

I'm Love. At one point or another, I am involved in every life. I either ruin them, or make them better. Every single moment of every single day, I fly around the world, watching people fall into, well, *me*. And every single day I watch people do the opposite of what I am for: Hate. That guy is no good. He still lives with his mother and runs around yelling at people all the time.

I live in the clouds, watching over humanity because

this is what I am meant to do. I worry about people and smile over them, and all the while they never know I am there. Some call me cupid. Some call me deception. At the end of this novel, the choice will be up to you. I watch over humanity and when I see two people who I think will better each other's lives, I make it happen. Think of me as the person that can make all the soap opera couples you secretly want to happen, happen.

There are many stories like that of young Romeo and his lover Juliet that I have been involved in. I have seen true romantics and those that fall short, *very* far short—and yet, thanks to me, they always get the girl or the guy. I bounce from couple to couple, from single person to single person. If you're still single, then it's either because you want to be, or because I'm really busy. I'll get to you eventually, I promise.

Today, though, today I am here for a very specific purpose. There is one story that has never been told, never been repeated or talked about for generations. You may know part of the story because it is a classic tale, but I promise you, you won't know all of it. Because this is all of it, the story of Hollywood's two hottest stars and how they fell in love and stayed in love against all odds. With a little help from me, of course. This story is one of my favorites because it reminds me why I am who I am, why I watch over people, why I guide them when I can, and stay away when I know I should. This story reminds me of everything I stand for: for people who search me out, a beacon of hope, something to cling to in a world where everything is temporary.

I come at strange times, I will say that. I come when I am least expected, when maybe you just got over a bad breakup and you aren't ready to move on, though trust me, if you broke up, I was *not* involved in the setting up. However, that is a whole other story.

Our story starts in December of 2023, two years before the first film in the *Aliens* series is set to be released. It takes place in Los Angeles.

I wasn't there for this whole love story. I was only there for certain parts, as I had other people to see, but the parts that I saw fascinated me, perhaps because these two particular people did things that I, me, Love, had never seen before. Maybe this was what encouraged me to keep coming back. Either way, it is a very good thing that I came back as often as I did, because otherwise you, dear reader, would be stuck reading this story in a few short pages in a trashy magazine article with all of the characters portrayed as either really good or really bad, and none of the truth actually there. Instead, dear reader, you would have had to put up with falsified events and exaggerated details, not that the participants in this story would care. They had long since learned that it didn't matter what the media said, that their lives would go on simply because they had each other.

I am going to tell you this story not because I think that this is how people should react when they, well, when they *love* each other, but because their love reminded me of why I do what I do. They reminded me that perhaps life isn't completely meaningless if you find someone to spend it with you.

And so, dear reader, pull up a chair, a blanket, and some hot cocoa because you are in for a very lovely story. Just remember, this story is for your ears only. Don't sell it to the media. I've found they typically corrupt everything good until there is nothing left of the old, of the truth.

CHAPTER TWO
THE PEOPLE

"The cast for the first film in the *Aliens* series has been announced. Yes, that's right, the cast that will be playing the characters from the *Aliens* book series, set to hit theaters in March of 2025, has been announced. The novel tells the story of Claire, a rebellious young girl from the future, who, along with her brothers Louis, Hudson, and Julien, travel to our time and get stuck. It is there that Claire meets her two best friends, Emerald and Rose, and the boy that she is destined to fall in love with: Rory. Just as most novels become films these days, we will see more than one teen heart throb and beauty queen. Joshua Clemons and Lucas Evans, the dynamic duo from *The Stars* films, are set to play Claire's brothers, along with Jamie Hughes from *Grassland*, while Michael Roberts from *The Promise* is set to play her love interest. As for the actress playing Claire, the feisty heroine who has inspired a generation, Hollywood is introducing a new star to the big screen: Amelia Alverson.

The film is set to be a big hit in the box offices. If it succeeds, then we will see the other five novels made into films also. You can expect that this will be the film story of a generation. Stay tuned for more up-to-date news right here at starcrossedlovers.com, until the next time."

"So have you heard?"

"Heard what?"

"The buzz about Joshua Clemons!"

"Hollywood's new *it* boy?"

"Yes! He's going to be playing Lewis in the new *Aliens* films!"

"This could do wonders for his career, I mean *wonders*. These books have one of the largest followings we have seen in a very long time. He's already big here in the States and, frankly, all over the world and he's only twenty-four! With these films, he may end up being the poster child of this next generation of heart throbs."

"Well, we will just have to wait and see but I am *very* excited to see what he has in store, I will say that."

"Amelia Alverson will be playing Claire. She has never been in anything in Hollywood, not just nothing big, but nothing at all. I am very interested to see how she handles the sudden wave of fame."

"Let's hope the directors were correct in casting her. Casting a nobody for a role like this could make her into a somebody, or it could destroy the films altogether."

"Well, we are just going to have to wait and see."

"Joshua, I know you are here to promote your new film, *Plastic*, but I have to ask about the *Aliens* film since the news just broke. Are you excited for that?"

"For my part, I am very excited to begin work on the film. I am a huge fan of the books and when I heard that they were going to be made into movies I called up Patrick Green, the director, and begged him to put me in it. I was very lucky that he obliged. I love the story that these books tell and I'm very excited to share it with people as well as present it in a different format to those who already know it."

"Thank you, Joshua. You and Lucas have been cast in the film together now that you've just finished filming *The Stars*. What was it like when you both found out that you had the roles?"

"We were so excited. Luc is honestly one of my best friends. I love the guy to death and the opportunity to work with him again. He's a great actor and nothing makes me happier than being able to tackle this project together. We're going to have fun with it and hopefully make a good movie in the process."

"You also have the pleasure to work with another

up-and-coming star like yourself: Jamie Hughes. Are you excited for that?"

"Jamie and I were both child actors so we saw a lot of each other growing up. He was great to work with then and I'm sure he'll be great to work with now. He is an incredible actor and it's a privilege to surround myself with such big names in the business."

"I believe that's all the time we have! Joshua's new movie, *Plastic*, hits theaters Friday! Thank you for your time, Joshua. Joshua Clemons, everybody!"

"Thank you."

CHAPTER THREE
THE CLUB

"They haven't called yet. Do you think that means that I won't get the part?" Joshua Clemons demanded of his best friend, Lucas Evans, over the loud pop music. It was some new contemporary singer that the boys didn't know and would never bother to. He raised his beer to his lips and sipped.

Joshua Clemons was Hollywood's hottest single man. Or at least, *now* he was single, and of medium height, with tousled brown hair, chocolate brown eyes, tannish skin, and firm build.

"I'm sure that's not it," Lucas replied.

His best friend, Lucas, had blond hair and blue eyes. He was taller than his companion, pale, and lean, another heartthrob. The boys were at a club talking about these callbacks for a very simple reason: not because they really deeply cared at this moment in time, but because Joshua had just broken up with his girlfriend of two years: Samantha Logan. She was not a celebrity but was a bratty girl who he had gone to school with in Tennessee. He had dated her this long because she wasn't from the world he was currently in, but from his past world. Needless to say, the two actually had nothing in common. It was a good thing that they didn't, too, because I had run out of time to visit Joshua before, but I was here now. Strangely enough, I had visited Lucas here one year before, when he met Eva Noble, his girlfriend. I really liked this club.

The bar was modernly furnished and set in an abandoned warehouse that some rich young billionaire had decided to put together to save face for his parents. I loved that family. The bar had flashing blue and green lights, attractive young women bartenders, and was known for its loud music, trendy clients, and exclusive crowds that lined up around the block to get in. Joshua and Lucas were usually some of the first let in. They had a reputation for being fun.

Joshua was from Chattanooga, Tennessee, a small city in the bottom of the state. He dressed like it: he wore a simple t-shirt, white, with blue jeans and short, dark green, combat boots. Lucas was from London, England. He wore a dark blue polo, blue jeans like his friend, and white converse shoes. Joshua had never been to college but had been acting since he was a child. Lucas had been to acting school and boarding school all the way up. He went to a very good university for acting there. The boys had virtually nothing in common, with different backgrounds and different hobbies. Lucas loved sailing and Joshua got seasick. Joshua was calm where Lucas was rowdy. Lucas was not afraid to speak his mind to get what he wanted while Joshua preferred to put others' priorities before his own. Yet their bromance had been intense from the day they had met, three years ago. They were completely and totally inseparable, probably because they completed each other perfectly.

"You know what? Whatever. Girls are stupid anyways!" Joshua exclaimed.

"Are you suggesting that we get roaring drunk and say things that we will regret in the morning?" Lucas asked.

"Yes!" Joshua exclaimed.

"That would be very amusing except for I can't tonight," Lucas said, sounding like he really meant it, too.

"Have you got something with Eva tomorrow?" Joshua asked.

"I'm meeting her parents."

"I want a girlfriend."

"I know you do, mate," Lucas said, patting him on the back.

"Or maybe I don't."

"That's fine, too," Lucas said.

"I don't. I never want to kiss a girl again."

I smiled. I would change that soon. I just needed to find the right girl for Joshua. Luckily for me, I would— very soon, too. I just didn't know it yet.

"You could go for guys now if you wanted to," Lucas said with a smile. He knew his friend well enough to know that Joshua would fall into love very soon and would soon be over Samantha. Joshua was an incredible romantic while Lucas was quite the pragmatist.

"I could and I might," Joshua affirmed.

"Who cares, anyways? Girls love you, mate. They scream your name every time you go out in public. You'll find someone else. I bet the next girl you meet will be the girl that you marry," Lucas said.

"You think?" Joshua asked.

"Sure," Lucas said.

Of course Lucas was right, though the first time Joshua would meet her, he wouldn't feel a thing. We'll get to that later. He wouldn't think anything of her until the second time he would see her, not even giving her a second thought until she would become the only thing on his mind for the rest of his life. I've always wondered if Lucas knew that when he said those words, or if he was simply trying to give moral support. Unfortunately, I can read emotions and feelings, but not minds.

Several things needed to happen in order for Joshua

22

to meet the girl he had always been destined for. At that club near that bar, surrounded by music and half naked drunk girls, that was when the pieces of the puzzle would start to fall into place. It would all start with the ring of a phone.

Joshua's phone vibrated in his jeans pocket. He pulled it out and swiped the screen, holding it to his ear.

"Hello?"

"Hello, is this Joshua Clemons speaking?"

"Yes it is," the young man said, immediately sobering up.

"I am calling on behalf of Patrick Green, the director of the *Aliens* film. You have got the part of Lewis."

"Wait, really?" Joshua asked, excitedly. "Thank you! Thank you so much!"

Click. The line went dead. There were more calls to be made, some hearts to break, some days to make.

"What was that all about?" Lucas asked when his best friend had hung up. Joshua stared at his phone in utter awe, as if shocked that it was capable of bringing him such intense joy.

"I got the part," he said, dumbfounded.

"You did?" Lucas asked, his face lighting up for his best mate. "That's brilliant!"

It was at that moment that Lucas's phone rang.

"Hello? Is this Lucas Evans?"

"Yes, this is him speaking."

"Hello, I am calling on behalf of Patrick Green, the director of the *Aliens* film. You have got the part of Hudson."

"Thank you so much," Lucas replied calmly.

Click. That line went dead.

Lucas was in shock. I smiled. He was destined to play a big part in the love story I was about to write out. To do that, he would need that part.

"Who was it?" Joshua asked, not sure how to react. It was always difficult to comfort someone after they had lost a role that they really wanted.

"The casting director," Lucas replied, his voice quiet amid the loud music and chatter of the club.

"What did they say?" Joshua asked, almost afraid to hear the answer.

"I've got the part," Lucas said, breaking into a smile of pure joy.

The boys celebrated and went home to tell Eva all about it. Little did they know it, but somewhere else someone else was also getting news of the casting...

"Amy, you have to take the role."

"Is this why you called me here today? You know I don't want it, Patrick. I can't even act," Amelia replied.
The two sat in a café. She drank hot cocoa, as she didn't like coffee, and he drank straight black coffee. He liked it simple.

24

Amelia was a moderately pretty girl with blond hair, green eyes, and skin a shade too white to be tan but a shade too tan to be pale. Amelia wore a dark blue sweater with white shorts and white converse. She was twenty-one but only just so. Looking at her, you would have thought her younger, but talking to her, you would have thought her older.

"You can, though. We've seen you," Patrick argued.

Patrick had chocolate colored skin, warm brown eyes, and a bald head. He was relatively thin for someone in his fifties. He wore a dark purple polo and white pants with brown shoes.

"You had me say a couple of words to the actors. It didn't matter, it wasn't a real audition," Amelia said.

"Amy, we've chosen you."

"Well then, legally I am allowed to decline. I know my rights and I read my contract. I can decline," she replied.

"Well then, I am allowed to resign," Patrick said.

"No, you aren't." She shook her head.

She had read his whole contract, through and through. Like I said: she was a sharp one.

"Then I am allowed to make this movie horrible. There was no clause that said it had to be a *good* film," he replied. He had known she would argue and had spent time coming up with counters.

"You wouldn't," she said, shocked.

"I would. It wouldn't be hard, either, since I would have to get someone else to play Claire," he said.

"I'm the writer, Patrick. People will think it's weird. They won't like it. I'm a nobody. You need big names for these roles," Amelia replied.

Perhaps I forgot to mention that Amelia Alverson was not an actress. She was a writer. It was she who, starting at the age of thirteen, had written the first book in the *Aliens* series. She had written all four books during high school, where she took three languages—English, French, and Mandarin—in addition to learning Italian and Spanish on her own time. She did theater, was on the school newspaper, did Model United Nations, was on varsity swim team, took higher level math and physics, and was generally just a smart kid. She graduated from her high school and went to Stanford University, where she was a junior and currently majoring in mechanical engineering and creative writing with a minor in psychology. She was no ordinary girl, as Joshua would find out. She had never had a boyfriend though, at least not in the real sense of the word.

She had met me once before, in the face of a young man who would steal her heart so completely it still shocks me to this day. She gave all of herself to him, mind, and eventually body. He broke all of it, disregarded it. She never spoke of it to anyone. She felt it was best they didn't know of what she considered a failure, a lapse in judgment, a showing of emotion. She had not been involved romantically since. That's not to say that guys weren't interested, that's to say that she didn't have time for them.

"They won't care that you're the writer, just so long as you play Claire well. And you *will* play Claire well," Patrick said.

"What about the other actors? On set? That will be so weird for them, being with the author of the characters they are playing on a regular basis!" Amelia exclaimed, desperate for a reason not to do the project. She didn't consider herself an actress despite several high school leading roles to her name. She had never wanted to get involved in all the chaos that was and still is Hollywood.

"Then don't tell them," Patrick said, simply.

"Don't tell them?" she asked, incredulous.

"Lots of times the authors don't get involved. They won't have searched for your picture on the Internet, I can guarantee you that. You'll tell them when they know you and it won't be weird," he suggested.

"I'm still in college, I'm much too busy."

"We begin filming the day you get out of school for summer. Talk to Stanford. They'll understand."

"I just can't."

"Look, it comes down to this: these are your books, your life. Do you want them made into a film correctly or not? Because if you do, then you have to take the role.

If you don't, which everything up until this point would dispute, then you can walk out that door right now and I will never bother you about it again," Patrick said.

Amelia was quiet for a moment and took a sip of her hot cocoa. She didn't want to do it, but her novels were incredibly important to her and she didn't want to see them sabotaged. Thus the trickster was tricked.

"I'll do it."

CHAPTER FOUR
LOVE AT FIRST SIGHT

In every relationship there is that moment when you meet the girl, where you've seen her many times before, so many but none of it matters, not really. Because when you see her, it just hits you. You know that that's the girl you want to spend the rest of your life with. That's when you know that I've been there, when everything else falls away and it's just you and that person. Joshua was about to learn what that was like.

"Joshua, mate, people are starting to arrive! I can't wait to meet our future set mates!" Lucas exclaimed, running up to Joshua and smacking him in the small of the back. Lucas could be restrained, calm, but around his friends he let his aloof personality drop. He especially trusted Joshua.

Joshua had decided to host a pool party at his house in L.A. before filming began, as a way to bond together. His house was beautiful, a white modern house with box upon box layered together and a pool with a water slide set in a large deck with a fire pit.

"That's great!" Joshua said.

His shirt was off, revealing his abs and also a tattoo of the Tennessee State college football team, an orange TN. He also had one on his wrist that was a compass with North, South, East, and West. On his back, right under the nape of his neck was a mockingbird, the Tennessee state bird, with its wings spread. This was about to get interesting, because his dream girl hated tattoos.

That was when Amelia walked in. She wore a dark blue dress, with a "v" shape in the front and a collar that was rather short in the back to cover up her one-piece, speedo, racing suit. Her blond hair was in a braid and the second she walked out onto the patio, she caught Joshua's eye.

Joshua looked at her and her smile as she turned to say hello to Michael, the handsome man who would be playing her love interest, and Joshua was in love. He just knew that she was the one. Looking at her, the world stopped and it was just the two of them.

Lucas, wearing grey swim trunks, looked where his friend was looking and said, "Well, that will be the girl that they've got to play Claire."

Joshua didn't even hear him.

"See that girl, Luc? That's the girl I'm going to marry. Excuse me."

With that, he ran off through the crowd to reach to her. He dodged through people, straining his neck to make sure that he didn't lose her from view. She was still talking to some random person that for that one shining moment was a criminal, distracting her from him. He finally made it to her and she looked at him and smiled. Her eyes never left his face to pursue his body, like most girls. The girl she was talking to walked away.

"I'm Joshua Clemons," he said, extending his hand.

"Nice tramp stamp." She ignored his hand completely and nodded towards the TN on his hip. She knew who he was and she knew he was hosting the party, not that saying what was on her mind had ever stopped her before.

"Um, actually tramp stamps are on your lower back," he said, looking down at the tattoo and silently regretting every decision he had ever made.

"Are they now? Good to know." She was smiling slightly and to him that made her all the more beautiful.

"Do you not like tattoos?" he asked.

"Not really, no," she said.

"Why not?" Girls typically loved tattoos. The whole bad boy vibe was very popular. His last girlfriend Samantha had loved his tattoos.

"Putting images on your body? That suggests that you aren't comfortable with the way it looks naturally," she said, shaking her head.

"Well actually I got this because—"

"Because you went to college there?" she interrupted.

"Well, no," he said, deciding on the spot that the moment this party was over he was going to sign up for classes online.

"Oh, you just like the school," she said, nodding. She was quiet for a while, teetering back and forth from her toes to her heels before saying, "I'm sorry, I've been horribly rude. I didn't really want to be here but there's no reason to take that out on you. I'm Amelia Alverson."

He broke into a smile, relieved.

"Nice to meet you, Amelia. Can I call you Amy?"

"I would love it if you did. Can I call you Josh?" she asked, smiling in turn.

"No one really ever calls me Josh, so yeah, yeah that would be great."

"You have a lovely house, Josh," Amelia said, gesturing around her.

"Thank you. Do you live around here?" he asked.

"No, I'm from Newport Beach, so I guess that's kind of close," she said.

"It is. What role have you got in the films?" he asked, as if he didn't know.

"Claire. You?" As if she didn't know.

"Lewis."

"I love Lewis, he's such a sweet sensitive guy. He loves Claire so much and would do anything for her," Amelia said, talking about what she knew.

"Well, she loves him, too. She nearly dies trying to save him," Joshua said, his voice getting animated in turn.

"That was great. Have you read all the books?" she asked.

"Yes, several times. I love the series. I think the books are phenomenal. The story that they tell is beautiful."

"You think?"

"Of course. It's a story about family and sacrifice, an instant classic. The author is a genius," he said, clearly not realizing who he was addressing. I knew, though. She certainly didn't tell him.

"So, what sports do you like?" she asked, changing the subject away from herself.

He laughed, "Um, I like soccer, basketball, baseball, hockey. What about you?"

"The same, minus basketball," she said, smiling.

"Really?" He was shocked. Most girls he knew didn't like sports unless it involved watching the guys on the court because they thought they were attractive. Of course, that might be why she liked them, too. He would have to wait and see. "What teams do you like?"

"In order: Barcelona and Manchester United, the

Giants, and the Sharks. I'm trying to get into football," she said, smiling slightly.

"Not bad." He smiled, trying to stop his heart from beating.

"Are you a Dodgers fan?" she asked.

"Yes."

"We can't be friends, then." The Dodgers were the Giants' enemies and had been for almost a hundred years.

He laughed. "So you're saying for this friendship to work out I have to change my preference of baseball teams?"

"That's exactly what I'm saying," she said, laughing.

"At least we know where we stand." He smiled.

"At least we do."

Lucas came running up behind Joshua. He had asked Eva to bring some of her hot friends to help get Joshua back in the game.

"Joshua, there are some ladies here to see you."

Amelia smiled, extending her hand.

"Nice to meet you. I'm Amelia. Or I guess Claire now."

Lucas glanced at Joshua. He could see the way that his best friend looked at her. Interview time.

"Hullo, I'm Lucas, but you can call me Luc. All my best mates do. I'll be playing Hudson. I don't recall seeing you in anything before. Please forgive me if I'm mistaken."

Amelia grinned. "You're not. This is my first job in

Hollywood."

"And yet you have landed the lead in one of the most talked-up film franchises of all time," Lucas said, looking her over.

"It would seem that I have. How very fortunate for me," she replied. Her eyes met his gaze rebelliously.

Lucas sensed her spirit and liked her. She would be a nice match verbally for himself, and he smiled genuinely at her.

"How very fortunate indeed."

Amelia smiled at him before turning to Joshua who had patiently been waiting for their conversation to resume.

"I think you have some girls to talk to," she said.

He turned around. There were three incredibly gorgeous girls in three very skimpy bikinis. They were tan and lean, stunning. He turned back around. To everyone else, Amelia would have looked pretty, but simple, makeup-free.

"I'm good here, thanks."

"Are you sure? They look very prepared for, well, for I don't really want to know what." She eyed them critically.

"Yeah, are you sure, mate? They're all very nice," Lucas said, trying to hide the fact that he wanted Joshua to stay with the nice girl.

"I'm sure," he said, smiling at Amelia.

Lucas winked at Amelia and walked off, pleased with the way the party was going.

"Does your boyfriend like sports?" Joshua asked in what he thought was a very sly manner.

"Well, he's imaginary so..." Amelia said, before laughing at the expression on Joshua's face. "I'm kidding, obviously. Smooth way to work that into the conversation, by the way, props to you. I don't have a boyfriend mostly because I don't want one. I'm super busy at the moment and if I ever had a boyfriend I would want to be able to concentrate on him at least some of the time."

The truth? That was a complete lie. She had time for a boyfriend. She was just afraid of having one, but we'll get to that later.

"Well, that's good to know," he said. Part of him wondered why he hadn't walked over to check out those girls but the other part knew that he would mentally be with Amelia even if he did. He was hooked.

"You can go check out those girls now. I won't judge you. I can help you if you want. There's nothing girls listen to more then the details of a guy told by a girl," Amelia said, smiling.

"Did you just offer to be my wingman?" he asked.

That was only *part* of her problem with guys.

"I like being the wingman. It's fun. Plus, if it makes someone happy then it's a win-win."

"I guess it is," he agreed.

"So which one did you want me to talk up?" she asked, eyeing the three of them discreetly.

"None of them. You may not want a boyfriend at the moment but that doesn't make you any less interesting to talk to," he said, smiling.

"I suppose we will be working with each other for a long time. We should get to know each other."

"Hopefully we will."

"Agreed. Hopefully we will."

Dear reader, they did.

Chicago Daily Radio Station, July 2026

"Do you remember the first time you two met?"

"Oh yes, I told you I liked your tramp stamp."

"And I had to explain to you what a tramp stamp was. The tattoo is on the front of my hip, *not* right above my butt."

"I'm still waiting for you to fall asleep on set to give you one that fits your description."

"What would it be of?"

"It would say 'Your name.'"

"Joshua?"

"No, like the words, 'Your name.' That way you can tell everyone that you have their name tattooed on your butt. How's that for an opening pick up line? Luc will help me, I have no doubt."

"Unfortunately, I have no doubt either."

"So you two really were friends from the get-go?"

"Ams?"

"I'd say so. We hit it off. He was a Dodgers fan, though, and I told him right then and there that would not work."

"Did you learn to accept it?"

"No, I became a Giants fan instead."

"He came to the awesome side where we win the World Series."

CHAPTER FIVE
THE GOLDEN TRIO

Looking at Amelia now, so put together, so strong, I couldn't help but remember the first time I had met her. She had been a teenager, writing her novels, working hard on them, her life consumed with them. The first time I met her, she was crying, sitting on her bed, talking to her characters as she worked out a scene. I had watched a tear fall down her cheek.

"It doesn't matter, none of it does. No one actually cares," she had said, putting her face on her knees.

She wrote and wrote and the homework, the classes, the after-school activities, the constant running around, it was enough to make any one person crack. Her parents were there of course, but you see, the thing about Amelia was that she had always been a great actress, weaving lies around her. She needed someone to tell her that it was going to be fine but nobody did because nobody thought she needed to be told that. The thing Amelia was just realizing is that her writing, the series she had written, it had all been a cry for help.

She had wanted her parents to be proud of her. She needed someone to comfort her, but watching her, she cried so silently, and so sadly, that it occurred to me that the poor girl had never been comforted as she cried. Those were tears of someone who knew they would get scolded for letting the tears fall.

Seeing the confident Amelia now, my heart broke. She wasn't really confident; she had just learned to cover up the brokenness and assume that no one really cared whether she lived or died. Amelia wasn't shying away from Joshua because she didn't want a boyfriend. She wanted someone to care about her more than anything in the whole world. She just knew that people don't like broken people and he would leave eventually, leaving her more broken than ever, more terrified of trust. She had given her heart to a man only to see it thrown back in her face in pieces. She had never gotten positive attention and it had affected her, affected who she was as a person because she no longer believed that positive attention was possible. Joshua would have to break that stereotype to win her over.

All I saw when I looked at her was that scared young

woman who wrote because paper was the only thing that would listen to her, the page wet with the tears that she hated herself for shedding. It was her only comfort.

Two weeks later, I was back for the read-throughs with the whole cast, anxious to see how this would all play out.

"I'm so glad you guys are all here for the read-through today. Shall we go ahead and get started?" Patrick asked.

Everyone was sitting in a circle. They had all met at Joshua's party, or at least most of them had. Amelia was seated with Joshua to her right and Michael Roberts to her left. Michael was tall with black hair and blue eyes. He was a very handsome, all-around good guy. He was also meant to play a part in this story. Amelia and Joshua just didn't know it yet. Lucas sat next to Joshua, and on Michael's other side was Jamie Hughes, Joshua's childhood nemesis.

"I hate that guy so much," Joshua hissed under his breath.

"Seriously, could he get more obnoxious?" Lucas asked.

I should probably explain. Jamie had a history of stealing roles that Joshua wanted, going all the way back to when they were children. Every role Joshua had ever wanted badly had been taken by Jamie. There was a lot of bad blood there. Jamie had brown hair and green eyes. He was tan and altogether very handsome. If he got Amelia instead of Joshua? It would be the last nail in the coffin.

"What guy?" Amelia whispered, leaning over to them.

"Jamie Hughes," Luc hissed.

"Half my friends have crushes on him."

"Then half your friends are idiots."

"I'll tell them you said that."

"Would you please?"

That's really how it went on. They read their lines and then they took to an old and time-tested method: passing notes. I intercepted some of their notes:

From Amelia to Joshua: *He seems really nice, though. I was talking to him earlier.*

From Lucas to Amelia: *DON'T BELIEVE A WORD THE BLOKE SAYS. HE IS PURE EVIL INCARNATED.*

From Joshua to Amelia, written under Lucas's note: *Exactly. The guy is bad news. Talk to him as much as you have to, nothing more.*

From Amelia to Joshua: *How bad can one person truly be?*

From Lucas to Amelia: *Do you really want to know how bad one person can be? Because let me tell you...* This was followed by a long list of reasons why Jamie Hughes was a disgusting, vulgar man, who killed puppies in his spare time (which I highly doubt) and a whole long list of other things that I will not begin to repeat.

That was how the three of them passed the entire read-through: reading their characters very seriously, with Amelia barely needing to look at the page because she had written the words, and Lucas and Joshua sending notes her way. I'm not going to pretend that Patrick didn't notice, but I'm also not going to pretend that Patrick was a strict man. They never missed a cue and were so good that he didn't mind. If it entertained them to pass notes, he was not going to take it away from them. That was really where their friendship began, in those passed notes, in those secretive grins that suggested that they knew something that you didn't, which they did. They knew each other.

Joshua had plans to ask Amelia to coffee. He knew what she had said, but he just couldn't get over her. Two weeks after their meeting, she was all he could think about. His plans were ruined, however, by her.

Amelia to Joshua and Lucas: *Guys, what are you guys doing tonight? We should do something fun. Cast bonding.*

Lucas to Joshua and Amelia: *Eva and I were going to watch a movie at home. Did you two want to come over and watch it with us? I already texted her to get her permission.*

Amelia to Lucas and Joshua: *What kind of movie are we talking? I don't do chick flicks.*

Joshua smiled despite himself: *I don't, either.*

Lucas to Joshua and Amelia: *Well I do, so get over yourselves. I'm joking, of course, we're going to watch Star Wars. The first one.*

Amelia to Lucas and Joshua: *I'm totally in.*

Joshua to Lucas and Amelia: *Let's do this.*

Dear reader, this is how what would come to be known as the Acting Dream Team first took shape.

Eva was a very pretty girl with long, wavy, brown hair and green eyes. She was tall, thin, and American. She was incredibly nice, went with the flow a lot, and was generally very funny. She and Amelia would someday be best friends, but this is the story of the first time they met. Eva was an actress in her own right.

"Evs, they'll be here in a moment! Do you need me to do anything else?" Lucas asked, running through their Los Angeles apartment.

"To calm down?" she asked, gently putting the flowers he had brought home earlier in a vase on their table.

Lucas and Eva had a beautiful, modern apartment down the street from Joshua's house. Joshua had purchased a house because he thought he wanted to stay in L.A. Lucas had rented an apartment because he knew that he would one day go back to England. The question was when. He would do everything in his power to get Joshua to accompany him but he would need a major bargaining tool if he were going to make that happen. Joshua loved where he lived.

"Evs, one more thing," Lucas said.

"Yes?" she asked, patiently.

"Joshua really likes this girl. They're not dating because she doesn't want a boyfriend, but he really likes her, so talk him up,."

"So, don't ask them if they're dating?"

"Don't ask them under any circumstance."

"But now I *really* want to."

"Shh, I know. Joshua will kill me if you do. They're here."

With that, the two of them ran to the door. Eva straightened her light blue skirt and white silk top and he unruffled his nice white shirt that went with his black pants. It was a movie night in, but they were having dinner with guests. They needed to be dressed to impress.

"Ready?" she asked, smiling at him.

He kissed her gently on the lips. "Ready."

The doorbell went off.

They threw open the door.

I'll spare you the introductions. I'll spare you the details of dinner. What they ate, what they said exactly, it's not important. What was important was what happened that night, what they learned about each other going forward. Amelia didn't drink. Joshua was afraid of spiders. Eva loved wine, though not too much. And Lucas,

45

well Lucas loved making people laugh. That night, among the film, amid the laughs and jokes, amid it all, something was born, the kind of friendship that never dies, the realization that the people you would be working with are some of the best people on this planet. You see, Patrick didn't just pick good actors; he picked actors who, when put together, would make each other better. That's what this group of people did.

"I can't believe the movie is just over!"

"There are more of these, right?"

"Are you an idiot?"

"Let's watch the next one!"

"I'm in."

And so, ladies and gentlemen, this group of four young, soon-to-be-megastars stayed up all night watching the *Star Wars* films, laughing, joking, falling asleep and getting mustaches drawn on them for their trouble. Watching them, they reminded me of what friends were. Especially in Hollywood, friends were the people who kept you sane, who brought you down a notch. These four young people would do that for each other and much more in the future. I couldn't wait to watch them shine.

"Were you guys friends the moment you met?"

Lucas laughed. "You know, I really do think we were."

Amelia grinned. "I think for every person, there are

those friends that you don't really know how you became friends, you just did. One joke and the next day you wake up wondering how you ever lived without them. Life is funny like that."

"Too serious, Ams," Lucas said, shoving her slightly in a playful sort of manner.

She laughed. "I had to give an introspective response. You wouldn't understand. You don't know what introspective *means*."

"Would you ever let anyone into your little clique?" the interviewer asked, leaning forward to hear their answers.

"We have a *clique*? I've always wanted a clique. Does this mean I can snap my fingers in a Z formation and you guys will come running?" Lucas said, excitedly.

"Luc!"

"It's not like the bat signal!" Amelia said with a laugh.

"You guys are like my L-Men. Charles Xavier had X-Men, I have L-Men. This is brilliant."

"Shut up," Joshua replied with a roll of the eyes.

"We are no one's men."

"I guess to answer your question: we would always be willing to let someone into the clique, if that's what you would call what we have. I'd call it forever friends, but anyways, they would have to learn to put up with us first."

"We're always willing to substitute Joshua out. We

are looking for applications!"

"Just for that, you can't have any of the doughnuts I bought."

"Oh honey, we already stole those and gave them to everyone here," Lucas said with a laugh.

"You're so clueless," Amelia added.

"They did, they were delicious," the interviewer said with a smile.

"I need new friends."

"No, you don't," Lucas and Amelia said simultaneously with a laugh.

He didn't.

CHAPTER SIX
STUNTS

"You could just ask her out."

"She doesn't want a boyfriend, Luc."

"Then make her want a boyfriend."

"Boys, we're rolling in four!" Patrick yelled, interrupting their whispered conversation.

"No problem!" Lucas yelled.

The boys were on set, waiting for Amelia's makeup artist to put the finishing touches on the scars she was supposed to have on her cheek. This gave the boys a few minutes to talk since their movie night the other night. Things had gone great. They had all highly enjoyed themselves, except Joshua and Amelia hadn't made out. For Joshua, that was the one disappointment from the night.

"Of course I could ask her out, but I don't want to make it weird on set. If she says no, then we can never really be friends," Joshua said, glancing around him furtively.

"It won't make it weird. Something tells me that you two will always be great friends," Lucas said, grinning.

"Look, whatever I have for her, it'll go away, no problem. It always does." Joshua said, shaking his head.

"Places," Patrick said, and the boys ran over. "Amy, last chance to not have to do the stunt. It's dangerous. We can always have your double do it."

"Pat. Stop. I can do it," Amelia said, sternly.

The stunt wasn't a great one. She needed to get crushed by a plaster rock, ideal work for a stunt double, as they didn't want Amelia getting hurt in any way. But, much like her character Claire, Amelia was incredibly stubborn. Trust me, she would do every stunt possible.

"Umm, Amy," Lucas said, "I mean, if it's dangerous."

"Luc, I'll be *fine*. Okay?" she replied, rolling her eyes with a killer grin.

"Okay," he said, putting his hands up.

"And, we're rolling," Patrick called out.

"Guys, look up," Amelia said.

"Claire—" Joshua started to say.

"Lewis!" Amelia shouted, pushing both him and Lucas out of the way as the boulder tumbled off the tree into the ground.

"Cut!" Patrick yelled.

"Ams—" Joshua said, rushing forward, ignoring the fact that the crew were the only people who were supposed to move the rock.

She pushed from underneath and Josh pulled. The crew backed off.

"Josh, I'm *fine*. It's a stunt," she said. He grabbed her hand and pulled her to her feet.

"I know, you've just never done a stunt before and I don't want you to get hurt your first time. That would be horrible," he said, trying to play it cool. Lucas face-palmed himself behind his best friend.

"It's a fake rock, Josh. I'm going to have to do a lot worse. Don't worry about me. You can't freak out every time I do one of these," she said, smiling.

"Yeah, I won't," he said, still trying to play it cool.

Amelia wasn't telling the full truth. True to form, she was hiding something. She had been diagnosed with scoliosis, a problem of the back, a curvature of the spine, when she had been younger. She stood straight, but there was a reason at that first pool party she had worn a dress over her swimsuit. She had worn a back brace for seven years in an attempt to rectify a problem that could not be rectified. She'd had surgery, opening up her back and sewing it back up. It was a place on her body that she would always feel vulnerable about. There was no real way to solve the problem, though. Her spine would never

51

be straight and her pain level would never be zero. She wasn't supposed to be doing stunts for fear of hurting her back. Patrick should have stopped her. The problem was he, like everyone else, was in the dark. She would keep the information from them, enduring the pain, until one day it would be forced out into the open.

Let me just take a moment to say that any other director would have yelled at Joshua. Any other director would have told him that he couldn't freak out and to move on. It was a good thing Patrick wasn't any other director. He had worked with Joshua several times and he knew the young man well. Well enough to know that Joshua had never, never in his life, done what he had just done. Patrick smiled. Maybe there was something there.

Filming was scheduled to last three months: the first two in studios in Los Angeles and the last month in France, where there would be a little bit of minor shooting in Paris and quite a bit in Normandy, the northern part of the country. I was most excited for that part because Amelia spoke fluent French. She had learned it as a child in an immersion school, and most of her closest friends were French. I was dying to know if she would tell the others.

The thing about making movies with your best friends is that it goes by so fast and you have fun. I skipped a lot of the shooting—I had other things to do—but I always ended up coming back. It was a good thing I did, too, otherwise I would have missed the intense pranking on set.

Amelia is clever, Joshua is devious, and Lucas, well, boarding school had taught him a lot. The pranking wars were very intense between the three of them, with alliances constantly changing and clever pranks being pulled. I will relate some of the best ones now. There were others of course—cooking pants in the microwave was too funny to resist—but these are the more outlandish ones...

"You want me to stand guard at the door?" Lucas asked, skeptical.

"Exactly. I'm going to climb in the skylight of his trailer when he's asleep and draw a fake mustache, then put some whipped cream on his hand and give that mustache some sweet volume," Amelia explained.

Lucas grinned. "You are a devious one."

She beamed. "Why, thank you."

"Why am I guarding the door?" he asked.

"In case I need to make a quicker escape. Pulling myself out will take a while. Three knocks on my side of the door and step aside," she instructed.

The thing about good girls, dear reader, is that they aren't necessarily good, they're just good at not getting caught, and Amelia *never* got caught.

Of course, Amelia could have as much fun as she wanted with this. While Lucas and Joshua never failed to attempt to prank her, they were just that: attempts. They had never actually succeeded. Her best friend of thirteen years had taught her all the antics of pranking and she was a pro, never failing to recognize a trap. It was best to side with her whenever possible, the boys and everyone else on set had learned. She was formidable.

Later that night, at around midnight, Amelia, dressed in all black with her thick blond hair pulled elegantly back into a ponytail, pulled herself up onto Joshua's trailer and crept towards the skylight. She had everything she would need in a belt around her waist. These were trailers, after all. There were no alarms. Lucas stepped in front of the door. Shooting began in six hours. Joshua would know this and be asleep by now. Amelia had slept up until ten minutes ago when her alarm had set itself off and she had escaped her trailer. She didn't have any scenes the next day, nor did Lucas. She could sleep in as long as she wanted to.

Pulling a screwdriver from her belt, she unscrewed the screws keeping the round skylight attached to the roof of the trailer and slid it off. She tied the long rope that she had attached to the bricked wheel of the trailer around her waist and slowly, like a rock climber, lowered herself in.

Joshua's trailer was understandably simple, containing a bed, a desk, a mirror, a bathroom, and a dresser. There was a small television facing the bed, still on ESPN—a Giants baseball game. Amelia smiled to herself. She was rubbing off on him after all. She turned her attention to him. He was indeed asleep. His warm brown eyes were closed, his face looked younger and softer, his brown hair was ruffled from the pillow, and his blanket was half off, revealing his legs. He slept in boxers, shirt off. She forced her attention upwards to his face.

Amy walked toward him, silent as a feather falling through the air. Stealth was a point of pride for her. She pulled out a black pen from her belt, one of the ones that could be erased with just enough water, and ever so gently traced a French mustache on his face. She stood back a moment to admire her handiwork and grinned. She loved everything French and had a habit of responding in French and swearing in French due to her choice of friends. She spent time with their families and was a regular little French girl. She had suppressed all of that, contenting herself with a nightly reading of the language and video calls with her best friend that lasted a long time.

She pulled out the whipped cream now and sprayed a bit on his hand before gently running her finger over his upper lip, sending chills through him. His whipped creamed hand reached up to touch his lip, smearing the cream all over his upper lip. Amelia silently laughed and pulled out her phone. She crept to the door, knocked three times, opened the door, then crept back over to Joshua, and promptly took a picture. The flash went off. It should have woken him up, but she would have been gone by the time he would have opened his eyes. She darted out into the night, shutting the door behind herself.

Joshua smiled and opened one eye, licking his upper lip. "Well played, Ams, well played."

Another one of my favorite pranks involved Amelia and Joshua teaming up against Lucas.

"Wait, so you want me to put this in his shampoo?" Joshua asked.

"Yup, just pour some in. It doesn't have to be a lot," Amelia said, beaming about her latest scheme.

"What is this going to do, Ams?" Joshua asked suspiciously.

"It may or may not turn his hair blue," she said, grinning.

"Wait, permanently?" Joshua asked, half laughing, half incredibly excited.

"No, no, he needs his blond hair for the film. It comes out with water. It's just colored dye. Makes him freak out a little and then the hair people will laugh at him before they wash it out," she said, smiling as she rubbed her hands together evilly.

"How will they know to wash it out?" Joshua asked suspiciously.

"I might have let them in on it," she said, smiling deviously.

You see, Amelia didn't actually *need* to let the boys in on her pranks. They weren't necessary to her incredibly well-thought-out plans. She really only needed her clever brain, but she included the boys because she loved watching them get into it, and they did get into it.

"Okay, how would you like me to do this?" Joshua asked. He was a very smart boy, now taking classes at an online university because he wanted to feel like he had as much education as Amelia did. She was smart and he wanted to be able to catch up. He didn't have to tell her or anyone else, as long as *he* knew he could do it, could succeed if acting ever fell through. He asked her for exact instructions because there were exact instructions to be given. She was meticulous in the best of ways.

"You asked, good, okay. I'm assuming you know what time he showers?" she asked.

"No."

She raised an eyebrow.

"In the morning, around six."

"So sneak into his trailer it is," she said.

"He and Eva are going out for dinner tonight." Joshua said.

"Perfect. What time?"

"I don't know."

Again with the eyebrow.

"Eight."

"Meet you at his trailer at nine."

"It's a date."

He wished it were a date.

They met at the established time, both wearing regular clothes, their dress code communicated via text message. Amelia walked up to the door as of it were her trailer, confident in her success in being able to get in. She pulled a paper clip out of her pocket and picked the lock in seconds, opening the door and pulling Joshua along with her, like they were going in there for other reasons. He wished again.

"How do you know how to pick locks so well?" he demanded once they were inside and the door was shut behind them.

"I don't like locked doors. I always have to know what is on the other side and they cramp my style, so I learned to fix that," she said, making straight for the bathroom.

He followed suit. Once in the tiny thing, she grabbed the bottle of shampoo balanced on the shower ledge, popped off the top and dumped in the contents of the food coloring she had brought. She twisted the top back on, put the bottle exactly where it had been, and, grabbing Joshua, pulled him outside, locking the door behind them. They had disturbed nothing and accomplished their goal. It had once again been an incredible success. She grinned at him and grabbed his hand.

"I haven't had dinner yet. Are you free? I was thinking Italian."

"I haven't had dinner, either. Let's go."

That was their first date, though of course Amelia never called it that. She called it "hanging out." It was a date. I want to be very clear in saying that it was definitely a date. They drove there in his car, he opened the door for her, the restaurant was romantic, there were candles. They joked about the candles, but that didn't make them go away. It was the first date she had ever been on, and she was wearing jeans and a t-shirt, no makeup, with her hair flowing around her face, as naturally beautiful as she could be. Let me tell you that Joshua examined every feature of her beautiful face that night, over and over again. She didn't know, joking about sports and pranking, but he was.

"Did you know that apparently low lighting actually makes people want each other more?" she asked, gesturing to the candles.

"I didn't." He didn't need the candles. He loved her enough as it was.

"I learned that in high school biology."

It wasn't exactly sweet talk, but they would get there. They just needed time. Like, a lot of time.

She could deny it all she wanted. It was a date in every sense of the word.

60

CHAPTER SEVEN
LATE NIGHT ESCAPADES

Jamie Hughes was a self-centered, Hollywood-made bigot, in every sense of the word. He was rich, and handsome. Girls wanted him almost as much as he wanted himself, and wanted to irritate Joshua, always to irritate Joshua.

It wasn't that he hated Joshua as a person. No, that would be too simple for his twisted mind. He hated him because Joshua never seemed to care what people thought of him, until Amelia came along, that was. Now the poor guy was the most self-conscious man in the world, seemingly always worried about what she would think of him. So, Jamie decided that he would exploit this weakness.

"Jamie? What are you doing here?" Amelia asked,

opening the door to her trailer. She had read about this guy in the tabloids—well, on the covers of them at the grocery store, at least. Jamie Hughes was a player, with a different girlfriend every week. She wanted to stay away from him.

"Can I come in?" he asked. His British accent was velvet as he pressed his body closer to hers, his face close to hers.

She stood her ground, not tempted by him in any way. The wall around her heart was high, too high for even the beautiful Jamie Hughes to climb. "I think you'd better stay right where you are. What can I help you with?"

"Well, I was wondering what you were doing tonight," he whispered into her ear.

"Not you, that's what," she said, taking a step back inside and starting to close the door in his face. He stuck his foot in the door and stopped her from closing it all the way.

"Joshua Clemons. You could do much better than *Joshua Clemons*. He's nothing. He doesn't even have a college degree because he's stupid and can't get one. He's not worth your time, and he has a crush on you, a full-on crush. He isn't worth the ground under your shoes. All I'm saying is that you could do *better, much* better," he said.

"No one could do better than Josh. Sit down and shut up, because your opinion of him in no way lessens my opinion of him. It only lessens my opinion of you. Go home and study your lines, James. You could use the practice," Amelia snapped, stomping on his foot. When he picked it up as a reflex, she slammed the door in his face.

"You'll be sorry. I know people who can ruin you," he hissed through the crack of the locked door.

"I don't think they can."

They couldn't, though Jamie would eventually come up with something much worse to drive Joshua and Amelia apart. For the moment, though, she was seething. She was fiercely loyal and any attempt at bad-mouthing her friends was very much her business. Jamie Hughes would pay for his mistake dearly, too. He just didn't know it yet.

The next few days were a virtual hell for Jamie Hughes. Amelia was not the kind of girl you would want as your enemy. She was planning something, he could tell—from the way she looked at him, from the way she was being overly nice to him and the way her words didn't match her eyes—he just didn't know what.

Lucas recognized something was up, too, and decided to ask her about it. He suspected it had something to do with Joshua by the way Jamie was looking at him with renewed hate, like he was a particularly bad meal that he had just eaten in the cafeteria. Lucas didn't want Joshua to ask, but he did suspect that he would want his friend to hear the answer, so, he knocked on Amelia's trailer and told Joshua to stand under the window.

"Luc?"

"Hey, Amy, can we talk?" he asked, standing awkwardly on the steps leading inside.

"What about?" she asked, keeping the door to her room mostly closed so that only her head peeked out.

"Amy, can we talk *inside*?" Lucas asked, nodding his head toward the inside of her trailer.

She looked like she was trying to decide whether or not she wanted to let him in. He could see it in her eyes. She was hiding something in there. A boy? Actresses had done worse, but then this was Amelia. "It's about Joshua," he said, hoping that would spark her interest.

"Okay," she said finally, swinging her door open and admitting him quickly.

The inside of her trailer should have looked like his, and it would have if it wasn't full of everything under the sun: hair dye, eggs, duct tape, food dye, nail polish, a tattoo machine, and a gallon of bleach.

"Amy, care to explain?" he asked, half amused and half worried as to what all of it was for.

The air seemed to leave her and her shoulders collapsed. "It's for Jamie."

"Jamie Hughes?" Lucas asked.

"Yes."

"Mills, this is intense," he said, using his nickname for her. Joshua called her Ams and Mimi. Luc called her Mills.

"I know."

"What are you going to use all this for?" he asked, still highly amused.

"Jamie."

"Yeah, I know, why? You've pranked Joshua and me loads of times but this stuff seems more, well more permanent," Lucas said.

"It's designed to be more *permanent*," she acknowledged. Lucas was one of her best friends. He would keep her secret.

"Mills, what did he say to you?"

"How do you know he said anything to me?" she asked, still not ready to tell him, though she knew she should be.

"Because this is scary, and you aren't a scary person. Well, sometimes you are, but you get my point," he replied.

Lucas had seen her angry before. It was the scariest anger he had ever seen from anyone in his whole life. Unlike most people who yelled when they got angry, and the vein in their temples pulsed, none of that happened with Amelia. When Amelia got mad, really truly angry, which was hard to do, the anger went to her eyes. Her beautiful, piercing, green eyes danced, like the grass during a thunderstorm. She would pierce you with those eyes, and would speak with her voice deathly calm, sending chills up and down your spine. It was incredibly terrifying in every sense of the word.

Lucas had only seen that when she had to be angry in a scene. It was harder to be mad about something that wasn't real. He didn't want to see what happened when she really got mad. He saw a glimpse of it now, though. Every time he said "Jamie," he watched the fire in her eyes dance. Whatever he had said, he had gotten under her skin. Lucas *never* wanted to get under her skin.

"It was about Joshua," she said.

"I guessed as much. That was why I told you I needed to talk about him with you, in case anyone was listening."

"Clever." So she told Luc, she told him exactly what Jamie had said and done, and Joshua heard the whole thing, all of the mean words used against him. He learned that Jamie knew he had a crush on Amelia, he learned that Jamie was out to get him. He learned *everything*.

"Wow," was all Lucas could say when she had finished.

Amelia walked to the door and opened it, glancing under her window where Joshua was crouched. "Get in here, you. I have really good hearing. A leaf rustles and I know it."

Ashamed of what he had done, Joshua climbed out of her bushes and walked around, up the steps and into her trailer where she promptly shut the door. He knew from her eyes that she hadn't been mad at him. The look of utter pity was drawn all over her face.

"I wanted him to hear," Lucas said, unsure what else he should say. "I thought you would say something else."

She didn't seem to have heard him. Her green eyes searched Joshua's face for the hurt that was there. She grabbed his face in her hands and met his eyes full on. "I don't care what he says. The fact that you don't have a college degree means nothing to me, *nothing*, and I know he was trying to push us apart with that crush thing. You would *never* have a crush on *me*."

"Why not?" he asked.

"Because guys never like me. Why would you be any different?" she said simply, letting her hands drop from his face. There was no self-pity in her voice. She sounded like she was stating a well-known fact. It broke Joshua's heart. He wanted to tell her that she was wrong but he was afraid of how she would react. Would she laugh in his face? Would she roll her eyes? He gathered all of his confidence, forming the words inside his mind. He started to say something but she interrupted.

"Will you guys help me get back at Jamie or will you just stand there staring at me?"

They decided to help her get Jamie back.

They talked her out of a lot of the more permanent things. They didn't want to get in trouble for this, so instead they did something much simpler. Jamie went out on a date with some random girl, just like he always did, and using Amelia's paper clip, they broke into his trailer. They stuck eggs in all of his clothes, every pocket of everything he owed, all of his bags, his bed. They stuck some food coloring in his soap and had Amelia write a letter supposedly from an ex-girlfriend about how he was such a horrible guy and left it in plain sight so when he brought his date back she would see it. Then they spilled nail polish all over his bed and the bathroom floor, and dumped dog poop in strategic places. The three of them also installed cameras so that they could watch him and laugh at his reaction. They were out of there in twenty minutes and then gone, like ghosts that no one had seen. It was impressive.

Lucas went back to his trailer that was near Jamie's to call Eva, leaving Joshua and Amelia to walk back to their trailers together.

"I want to thank you for what you did," Josh said, smiling at her under the moonlight. She wore a sweater over a dark blue fitted tee, along with ripped skinny jeans and short boots. She looked beautiful.

"I didn't do anything," she said. He wore a striped blue and white t-shirt along with light brown khaki pants and loafers. It was February in Los Angeles, after all, you didn't need anything heavy duty.

"Yes, you did. You said so yourself. All of your friends have crushes on him which means that you probably did too, at some point, and yet you yelled at him and slammed the door in his face," Joshua replied, smiling at the thought.

"No."

"No?"

"No, I never had a crush on him. Movie stars are tricky. They're very good actors. You never know if they really like you or if they're just playing you. I never wanted that, but then I guess that now if any guy wants me, it's for my money or to be in magazines. I guess I kind of messed up my life," she said, smiling sadly.

"Hey," he said, nudging her arm with his. "Any guy would be lucky to have you, movie star or not. You're a great girl, and an even better friend. Tonight demonstrated that, if nothing else. Someday you'll find the perfect guy and he'll never have to act in love with you. You might have to act in love with him, but he'll never have to act in love with you."

She laughed and smiled at him, shaking her head. "When did you become my best friend?"

"Probably when you asked me about my tramp stamp," he said, smiling.

"It *is* a tramp stamp, you know that, right?" she asked, laughing.

"It's *not* a tramp stamp! It's on my hip!" he exclaimed, laughing.

"Exactly!"

69

"Do you even know what a tramp stamp is?" he asked, smiling.

"Of course!"

"A tramp stamp is on your lower back, right above your butt. Mine is on my hip in the front!"

"Same difference!" she exclaimed.

"Who says that? Seriously, who? It's 'the same thing'!"

"I knew you would be one of those people."

"What?"

"I knew you would be one of those people that saying *same difference* would annoy!" she exclaimed, laughing harder now.

"Well thank you for type-casting me!"

"You are very welcome."

Patrick Green smiled and stuck his head back in his trailer, shaking it all the while. There was something there. Amelia just didn't know it yet. But much like how he had convinced her to take the part, he would convince her to go on a date with Joshua. Life was too short to pretend like you didn't like someone.

They continued like this, going back and forth, making each other laugh, for a long while until they had reached her trailer and they separated, regrettably.

Comic Con Panel, July 2026

"First question is from Juliana Levy from Kentucky and it's for Amelia."

"In your face, boys!"

"What?"

"What? Nothing." She laughed. "Sorry, what's the question?"

"Favorite song?"

"That's easy. 'Searchlight' by Thomas Matthews."

"Really?"

"Yeah, the lyrics to that song are perfect."

"Okay, next question is for all three of you. Who was the best with pranks on set?"

"Ams."

"Mills, definitely. She's the master."

"What was the best prank she pulled on you two or anyone else on set?"

The three of them shared a look, a momentary glance that decided exactly how they would answer the question.

"She turned my hair blue."

"She gave me a French mustache and made me smear whipped cream all over my face."

"Um?"

"I was asleep. She snuck in my trailer and did it, but I didn't notice the next morning so I went to makeup with it all still on."

"It was one of my funnier pranks, really."

"She also cooked my pants."

"She cooked your pants?"

"I feel like I should explain."

"You probably should."

"Okay, so Luc was planning on wearing these specific pants on his date with Eva—"

"My girlfriend."

"—his girlfriend—but Josh and I are super good friends with Eva, so we decided that she wouldn't get mad at us if we messed with him before their date. So basically we found the pants he was going to wear, stuffed them in a microwave, heated them up, pulled them out and let him put his hot pants—"

"—literally *hot* pants—"

"—on."

"That sounds hilarious."

"It really was. He was dancing around his room jumping and yelling our names and trying to get them off."

"They were really hot!"

"One of the best moments of my life."

"We don't hold any grudges, though. That was the fun part about being on that set: no one held any grudges, everything was up for grabs, literally anything. I mean there were some lines we couldn't cross—"

"—like murder—"

"—like murder—but it was all just sport. It brought

everyone closer together."

Lauren and Tessa in the Mornings, Chicago, 2026

"Any advice on how to survive as the big Hollywood starlets that you are?"

"In the end, it doesn't matter what people say because only you can make what they say matter."

"My really good mate, Matt, used to say, 'Don't let it get to you. If something goes wrong, just leave it out of your autobiography...'"

"Don't get caught doing meth."

"Seriously, Luc?"

"I mean it's really good life advice, really."

Jamie Hughes never told anyone about the eggs in his trailer or his purple hair or any of it, not because he cared about them—he didn't—but because they all had one instruction from the production team, the same instruction each film actor got before the press tour for their film began: "You guys are all friends to the very end. I don't care what you say a year from now, when the film has left theaters and people have already bought the DVDs. I care about now."

Some groups of people, like Joshua, Amelia, and Lucas, didn't have to act. They really were best friends. But people like Jamie and Joshua had to make nice for the cameras at all times.

CHAPTER EIGHT
PARISIAN NIGHTMARE

Paris in March is freezing, possibly one of the worst places to be. There is no snow, but that's because it is physically too cold for snow. Instead, you get the frigid cold where the air feels thin but sound travels slower and you can't leave your house without twelve coats. Where is it colder than Paris in March? Easy: the northern part of France, or Normandy. This is where our lovely cast went to continue shooting the movie.

Amelia hated the cold. She had a very low tolerance for it and usually got cold around eighty degrees Fahrenheit. Lucas actually loved winter and the cold nipping at his skin. And well, Joshua, he didn't love it, but he didn't hate it, either. In fact, he loved sitting in front of a fireplace and watching movies with a blanket. He loved watching it rain outside knowing he was warm inside. He liked watching the cold, not so much being cold. He did have more of a tolerance for it than Amelia did, but then almost everyone did.

While in Paris, the actors were given a translator—well, two of them—for everyone on the whole set to use. Patrick knew that Amelia spoke French. It was just everyone else who was in the dark. Consequently, when Amelia, Joshua, and Lucas got a day off, the boys asked for the use of the translator to take the train to Paris to sightsee for the day. Patrick told them that they didn't need a translator and to have fun. The boys were confused but determined to go, so with Amelia in tow they jumped on a train, neither of them noticing that Amelia had purchased their tickets in the same amount of time it had taken every other French person there while they had stood to the side.

"Do you speak any French, Ams?" Joshua asked as they took their seats on the train.

"I took some in high school," she said with a shrug.

"So I'm assuming that's code for not really," Lucas said, with a laugh, Amelia just shrugged again.

She had her reasons for not wanting anyone to know the number of languages she spoke. Typically, from the time she was little, whenever people found out how many languages she spoke, it consumed their friendship with her. They would call her Frenchie, constantly tease her about how smart she was, and about how she probably didn't have any other American friends. She hated it. It usually helped her make friends because people thought it was cool, but she wanted to see if she could make friends and be smart without people knowing she had been a teenage writer or that she spoke so many languages. So far she had been pleased with her success. She would use her French whenever she could because she loved it so much, but she wouldn't use it in front of the boys.

"Well, bad is better than none. I don't know any. Luc?" Joshua asked.

"Like three words. I didn't pay much attention in that class, no one did. The Brits don't like the Frogs. Too much history and bad blood there," Lucas replied.

Amelia smiled. Wasn't that that the truth. She'd learned about the bad blood for years in history class.

"So I guess that makes you our translator!" Joshua said, smiling broadly at Amelia. He didn't know how easy the job he had just given her was.

"I'll do my best," she said, smiling, excited by the prospect of speaking French and seeing Paris again. She had been before but it had been a long time.

"What should we see?" Joshua asked. None of them had a guidebook, but they didn't need one. Amelia had done some "research" on stuff to see, which actually involved nothing, just remembering all the fun places to go from when she had been the other two times.

"We should go see Versailles, the palace of the French royal family, the Arc de Triomphe made for Napoleon, obviously the Eiffel Tower, and that will probably be all the time we have," Amelia said.

"Can't wait. It's been a long time since I've been here," said Lucas. Lucas had been here a long time ago. Joshua had only been for movie premiers and had never gotten to see anything.

Pretending her French wasn't very good worked all day. She would always tell Lucas and Joshua to stay where they were while she went and resolved the problem and they would, never noticing that she asked whatever their question was in perfect French. It all worked really well until they got to Versailles, where, as they were freezing and walking amid the splendid gardens, a handsome young Frenchman came running down the lane yelling for a doctor.

Amelia swore in French under her breath. She wasn't a doctor but she did know CPR and basic medical things. Lucas and Joshua looked horribly confused but chose to follow her, speeding through the garden after the young man, through bushes and trees and passageways until they came upon the largest fountain in the center, with Apollo, the god of medicine, and his chariot. In front of this basin an old man lay heaving, severely lacking in oxygen, clutching at his throat, surrounded by a group of concerned people.

Amelia knew that these people didn't speak English. The young man had a South of France accent, and she guessed that their English would be poor. So much for pretending her French was. She ran to the man and laid him out on his back in seconds and began giving him mouth to mouth. Joshua and Lucas looked on in shock. Slowly but surely the man's heartbeat picked back up. He had been having an asthma attack and no one in his family had known he had asthma.

The minute his heartbeat was closer to normal, Amelia began to give orders. She was a leader in all senses of the word. One young man was sent to get water, another a chair, another to call for help from the hospital. The entire time, the boys stood there, unable to digest her perfect French and the fact that she had just saved a man's life and didn't seem perturbed by it at all.

When everyone had run off on all their tasks and there were only a few people left milling around, Amelia began to speak calmly to the man who was incredibly amazed to find out that unlike her friends, who looked the picture of Americans even though Lucas was British, Amelia spoke perfect French. To calm him down, she told him all about her education, how her parents were American. He was fascinated. All the while she had him taking long, steady breaths as she kept speaking eloquently but using a few words of slang here or there which only seemed to delight him more. She had learned at a young age that the French loved it when you spoke French.

Finally she glanced over at her two confused companions and broke into a smile. "You two okay?"

"You said you had high school French!" Lucas exclaimed.

"Actually I said that I had French *in* high school, I just didn't mention that it followed the program for high school kids in France, or that I took French in middle school and grammar school too. You didn't ask about that," she said, smiling.

"What else have you not told us? How many languages do you speak?" Lucas asked, shaking his head.

"A few," she admitted. "French is probably my best, though."

"But your French... but you sound like a little French girl!" Joshua exclaimed, completely baffled by what he saw before him.

The young man who had come running for help earlier smiled. "She acts like zee little French girl!"

Joshua couldn't help but feel uncomfortable with the way the young man looked at Amelia. He poked Lucas. "He looks at her like... like..."

"Like he would do her right here?" Lucas asked, smiling despite himself, though he didn't like the guy's look of pure adoration, either. Amelia seemed like his little sister and he was a *very* protective big brother.

"Exactly."

"Boys, just because they don't speak English doesn't mean I don't," Amelia said, rolling her eyes at them, "and no one is getting done anywhere. We have to leave soon, anyway. I just want to get this whole thing settled first."

That was their first taste of how Amelia liked to save people. It wouldn't be their last.

"Is there anything else about you that I should know?" Joshua asked, amused. He was lying down on the bed of Amelia's hotel room while she paced, attempting to memorize her lines for the next day.

She stopped pacing and looked up from the paper, confused. "What?"

"I mean, you never told me that you were fluent in French and yet apparently that's a huge part of your identity. Is there anything else I should know about you?"

"That matters? Not really, no," she replied, looking back down at her script and resuming her pacing.

"Or that doesn't matter. Just anything about you that as your friend, I should know," he replied. His voice was nonchalant but his eyes told a different story.

She stopped pacing once more and looked at him. Usually he didn't talk when he came over to learn his lines and then run them. Usually he was quiet until they both knew their lines. It was odd, but she decided to indulge it. "Nothing that springs to mind, no. I'm not secretly an alien. I don't turn into a canine on the full moon. I drink no one's blood. Pretty normal."

"This is Hollywood. No one is normal," Joshua pointed out.

"What is up with this sudden desire to know more about me?" Amelia asked, curiously, not arguing with his statement.

"You're one of my two best friends. I just think that I should know more about you. That's fair, right?" he said, sitting up.

"We live in a bubble. What could you possibly not know about me that the press doesn't already have millions of articles written up about?" Amelia asked.

"I don't know, the mundane things. I don't know your favorite color, I don't know what your hobbies are, I don't know why you ever decided to be an actor." She opened her mouth and he held up his hand. "I know what you say in interviews, but I want the truth."

"What I say in interviews is the truth. I hate lying, even to sleazebags like some of the people in the media. My favorite color is blue, but light blue, none of that dark stuff, because it reminds me of the ocean, of where I grew up. In my spare time I love to swim, to dive under water and see how long I can stay there, shut off from the world. I love to read, to go to a different universe and live there for a while. As to why I became an actress, I suppose because I wanted to see this movie, the movies that we are doing right now, done right. I wanted to see them become what I had imagined them as while reading. I guess I thought I just might be the best person for the job."

Joshua nodded, smiling slightly at the progress he felt he had just made. They were simple questions, really simple, but there was something special for him in their answer, in this truthfulness meant only for his ears. "See, that wasn't so hard, was it?"

She rolled her eyes, "I never said it was going to be hard, I just said that I didn't understand why you wanted to know. Now it's your turn. I think I know the answers to the last two, so what is your favorite color?"

"Wouldn't you love to know?" Joshua asked with a grin.

"Not cool!" Amelia said with a laugh.

"Google me. I think you'll find I am the very definition of cool."

It was five months and a promotional tour later.

"Hey Ams, do you have advice on how to woo a girl?" Joshua asked in what he hoped was a very nonchalant way. The two sat in the back of a car that would take them from their last interview back to their homes for the evening. The Los Angeles premiere was in two days.

"Depends what kind of girl."

"The really quiet, sweet and smart kind."

She looked out the window at the city that flew by

and smiled. She didn't know it was her. "Well, I should think buying her a copy of one of her favorite books and annotating it with what he thinks, and then giving it to her. That way she is closer to him, and she understands him more, which I think is important."

"Thank you. I'll try that."

"Amelia, we have a slight publicity thing we need you to do."

"Okay, what?"

"Well, actually you don't have a choice. You have to do it; your contract binds you," Patrick said, sadly.

"You see this? This is why I wanted to stay away from all of this, from Hollywood! I mean, is there anything real about the people here? Does anyone actually care about who they are away from the cameras? I have to pretend to love someone that I don't because someone else is telling me too. How dreadfully *ancient*," Amelia hissed.

"Welcome to Hollywood. You don't have a choice."

"What is it that I have to do?"

Joshua opened the door of his L.A. house to find Lucas standing in his bathrobe. In his other hand, Joshua clutched his annotated copy of *The Great Gatsby* by F. Scott Fitzgerald.

"Luc?"

"It's Amy."

"What's happened? Is she okay? Come inside!"

Lucas did. He had just run down the street to Joshua's house immediately after hanging up the phone from a conversation with Amelia. The Los Angeles premiere of their first movie in the series was in an hour.

"Nothing bad happened to her. It's just they want her to do a promotional stunt for the film. Apparently they've already been talking it up to all the magazines. We've just been ignoring them." It was their policy to ignore all gossip magazines.

Joshua let out a breath he didn't know he'd been holding. "Well, what is the stunt?"

"She's dating Michael."

Reader, you remember Michael Roberts, right? Amelia, Joshua, and Lucas's costar? He played Rory, Amelia's love interest in the films. He was tall and had black hair and blue eyes. He was a great guy, and even though he didn't mean to be, he was about to become the bad guy in our little fairytale. I told you he would play a part in this story and this was it.

"What?" Joshua demanded.

"Mike plays her love interest and the producers think the movie will get more hype if the romance is, or at least seems to be, real." As if Joshua didn't have to watch her kiss Michael enough on set, knowing that he himself could only ever play her brother, now he would have to do it in his daily life too.

"That's ridiculous."

"Think about it. It makes sense. If they were going to have her date someone then it would be him. He *does* play her love interest. They can't have you or Jamie do it because you two play her brothers. That would be weird for the audience. They want to know that we think of her as a sister, which I do. You don't." He took a deep breath. "Look, I'm sorry, mate, but you know how this business works. It's not as if you've never had to pretend to date someone to promote a film."

"How long do they have to pretend to date?" Joshua asked. There was nothing he or she could do about it. Plus, it wasn't like she had wanted to date him, anyway. To his knowledge, at least.

"I don't know, until they tell them that they are allowed to break up. Look, Mike had nothing to do with it. It was all the producers. Amy called to ask me if they could do something like this, make her date someone. I told her that they could. That they do, all the time," Lucas said, running his hand through his hair. "Her first boyfriend and he isn't even *real*."

Joshua didn't like this. He didn't like it one bit, but there was nothing he could do about it. He wouldn't give up. He would lobby the producers for a big breakup, that was for sure, but for the moment he just needed to get ready for the premiere.

"Okay, thanks for telling me. You should finish

getting ready. I'll see you at the premiere in an hour."

"Hey Joshua, mate, why are you holding a book?" Lucas asked, glancing down at the book in his friend's hands. Joshua read, but this wasn't really the time.

"It's a long story," Joshua said.

"Amy isn't even going to be wearing makeup," Lucas said with a smile. "She hates it. I've never seen any girl do that before."

Neither had Hollywood, neither had Hollywood.

When Amelia showed up at the premiere on Michael's arm, Joshua stopped dead. Not because she was on Michael's arm, though that did make him want to commit murder, but because she looked stunning. She wore a long, silk, strapless black dress, which was tight in all the right places, with her light hair tumbling around her shoulders and a very simple cross necklace, a gift from her grandmother, around her neck. It was true that she wore no makeup, but under the bright lights of the camera, where many would have felt exposed, her eyes met his and they shone brighter and more spectacularly green than ever. There was something in them though, a sort of wall, a barrier, separating him from her, from her thoughts. He would have given anything to get a look at her thoughts. She would have given anything to make sure that he didn't.

She made her way over to him and let go of Michael

for a moment to give him a hug. Michael shook his hand. Joshua tried to resist breaking it. "You look so handsome, Josh," she said.

He wore a tailored black suit with a black tie, keeping it simple. He did indeed look handsome, though. She wasn't wearing heels, unlike every other girl there, so she was still shorter than him by an inch or two. Part of him wondered if she knew she would be taller in heels and so she hadn't worn them. That part was correct.

"You look amazing, Ams. That dress looks killer on you."

"Thank you. Eva helped me pick it out." She beamed.

He smiled. Of course Eva had. He needed to remember to thank her later for that. Looking at Amelia, he imagined the life that they could have together: their wedding, their children, their grandchildren, all of it. He realized right then and there that he would never be happy unless he knew her, really knew her. He could never be close enough, could never understand her enough, to satisfy him. There could never be anyone else because no one else was her, no. No one else would make him happy like he knew that she would. In his mind she was his, completely and totally his, but reality was not his mind and in reality, nothing was further from the truth.

"How did the book thing work out for the girl you liked?" she whispered so that the screaming paparazzi wouldn't hear.

"I decided to give up on that. She's with someone else now."

"I'm sorry. There'll be other girls though, I'm sure," she said, gently, doing her best to hide the relief that she felt not only from Joshua but from herself.

She turned away and he murmured, "I don't think so."

The lights flashed in their faces, illuminating them to each other. Amelia blinked to get the shine out of her eyes. Joshua didn't. He didn't need to.

Lucas smiled at Amelia. She did look great. She beamed at him. He turned his attention to Michael and gave him a look that said *break her fake heart and I break your real face.*

89

CHAPTER NINE
FUTURE HOME

Amelia loved England. I mean really *loved* England. She watched British television, read novels set in England, used British words, built British monuments out of Legos, knew everything about the Royal Family, and worked on her British accent constantly, but could never really get it. Lucas loved it. They could talk about his homeland for hours while Joshua occasionally said something about the queen. That was all he knew. Consequently, it was no surprise that part of her novels were set in London, England, which naturally meant that the cast would do a bit of filming in Cardiff, Wales, an hour or two away from London.

Lots happened in the month before they got off the plane in London from the L.A. premiere of their first movie. The movie had been an incredible success, earning hundreds of millions of dollars at the box offices. Our three favorite leads had been thrust into the spotlight, and become household names. It was now much harder to leave their houses and do their normal things without being followed by the paparazzi. It bothered them, but not an enormous amount. Their comfort was that they all understood each other. It was a problem they shared which only brought them closer together. They were trapped, as they had all signed for any number of movies that were required by the film company, so they might as well make the best of it together.

Amelia dealt with celebrity differently than Joshua and Lucas. She didn't exactly try to fight it, but she didn't exactly completely accept it either. The celebrity still surprised her but also annoyed her. She wasn't going to take the harassment lying down from the 1% of people who didn't like her, especially not in the earlier days, the days before she truly understood what being a celebrity meant. Being a celebrity meant you were an easy target and measures needed to be taken.

One time, a man made the mistake of attempting to break into her house while Lucas and Joshua were over and the three of them were watching a movie late at night. They were all supposed to be away for the night at Lucas's Malibu house but had been too tired to make the trek and had just stayed in L.A. and decided to watch a horror movie. The break-in went a little awry.

The man, a young, heavyset individual covered head to toe in black, broke into the back door of her house at three o'clock in the morning with an axe. Of course the sounds that this axe made to open the door perfectly correlated with the movie sounds so not one of the actors noticed until the man walked into the living room, clearly not anticipating company.

Amelia jumped up from the sofa and turned around to face the man. Lucas and Joshua stood up behind her. "*What* do you think you are doing in my house with an axe?"

"Amelia—" Joshua started to say, putting his hand out in front of her, worried that she was not taking the situation seriously enough.

"No, Josh, we need to talk about this. I'm going to ask you again: what are you doing in my house? Are you here to steal some memorabilia to sell on eBay or something?"

"Uh," was the all the man could get out, so shocked was he that she was standing up to him when he had the axe and she did not, and that she was home in the first place.

"Did you not think I would be home? Well, you know what? No. Just *no*. If you are going to break and enter into my house you will *not* forget to do your research beforehand and come barging in when my friends and I

93

are trying to watch a movie, axe in hand, like a blubbering idiot! This is unacceptable, completely unacceptable. Do you hear me? Get out of my house this instant!"

The man was in complete shock. Every nerve he had used to break into the house dissipated as she faced him down. "I'm sorry?" he suggested.

"Well, you should be. It's just plain *rude*, that's what it is. You can grab some food on your way out from the kitchen—I think there is a leftover pizza that you can have in there if you need it—and forty bucks in the coffee mug next to the fridge that you can have, but after that there can be no more of this. There can be no more breaking into my house, especially when you don't even have the decency to check my Twitter before doing it. Now, out!"

The man nodded and backed out, worried she was going to follow him and keep yelling, worried that she wasn't going to follow him, worried about everything that had just happened. He didn't grab the pizza or the forty dollars.

"Did you seriously just tell an axe murderer to get out of your house and grab frozen pizza on the way?" Lucas asked when they heard the man leave the house and had checked that he was gone.

"It was only a day old; it was still good. It was a cheese pizza too, a pretty universal flavor. I can't believe he didn't take it," she remarked, checking the fridge and seeing that he had not taken the pizza. "I don't think he was an axe murderer, either, just some fan trying to amass a mound of tissues I've blown my nose with."

"He had an axe and you're upset because he didn't take your pizza? Amelia, you don't need to play an action hero in a movie, action heroes need to play you in real life."

George Newark Show, 2028

"Weirdest piece of merchandise for the film?"

"The dolls."

"Why the dolls? They make dolls for almost every popular movie!"

"Yeah, Mills, why the dolls? I would have gone with the underwear! I mean those are almost *too* personal."

"Because it's me, but in mini, and it's you two, but in mini, and it makes me uncomfortable that people can literally *play* with us."

"Joshua?"

"I like the dolls, I think they're funny. I agree with Luc, the underwear is creepy."

"You're creepy, that's why the underwear is creepy. They can't help it with your face on them."

"Love you too, Ams."

"I know you do."

"I still don't get why you don't *adore* London, Josh," Amelia said, pulling her carry-on out from the overhead bin. She had sat next to Joshua the whole flight to London with Lucas on his other side.

"I *do*, I just like home, too," he said, shouldering his own carry-on.

"Do they have British accents at home?"

"Well, Lucas has an accent."

"But does *everyone* have a cool accent?"

"No."

"Do we have great television?"

"Yes."

"Reality television is horrible. I don't care that it's your guilty pleasure. You're guilty of watching horrible television."

"Well said, Mills."

"Thanks, Luc Skywalker. Now, do we have an incredibly old history with old buildings intertwined with new ones?"

"No, but we have liberty and no ruling class to bow to," Joshua said. His two friends just shook their heads.

"The UK is still superior."

"Whatever, I'll never live here," Joshua said as Amelia grabbed her things and began to walk off the plane. He followed with Lucas behind him.

"I will!" Lucas said behind him.

"I will, too!" Amelia said in front of him.

"Your two best mates will be here. You're living here, mate, I don't care what you say," Lucas said, nudging him in the back with his bag.

"London in February? You guys will change your minds real fast and you'll go running back to L.A.," Joshua said, sure of himself.

"I grew up here," Lucas said as they entered the terminal to camera phones and paparazzi, the clicks echoing around them. It didn't faze them.

"People don't know us as well here either, which is nice," Amelia yelled over her shoulder as she stopped to sign a young girl's copy of the novel. In America, the three could hardly leave their homes to go pick up groceries without being accosted, followed, or demanded for attention. Amelia dreaded the attention, but was as stubborn as ever in her attempt to maintain a somewhat regular life. Unfortunately for her, signing autographs would forever be her regular now.

"I've got to give you that one," Joshua said.

The security guards circled around them, something which always annoyed Amelia, and the boys saw the muscles along her jaw contract. She wasn't allowed to tell them to stop, but she hated it, despised needing a guard to go places.

"Plus, L.A. is just plain weird," Lucas said, as they walked through the airport to a waiting car. They weren't supposed to get their baggage because the crowds would be intense around them. Another muscle jumped in Amelia's neck. She hated having things done for her.

They exited the airport. A cold gust of air hit them in the face. Amelia ignored it, though there was a slight tremor in her muscles. She got cold so easily and there was snow on the ground and more coming down. Joshua fought the urge to bring her close to him to warm her up. She wouldn't like it.

Amelia continued, completely oblivious to his sentiments, "Plus, ever since I was a child my dream life involved living in London, in a house on Baker Street because my bedtime stories were Sherlock Holmes when I was a kid, and I would work on my favorite British television show, and I would take the train every weekend to Manchester to watch Manchester United football matches. I've always wanted to live here. I love the States, I do, but every moment I'm there feels like a moment wasted because I could be here."

They jumped in the black sedan with tinted windows and the driver started the car and began to drive.

"I always thought I would live in Los Angeles or in Tennessee and I would have a family with, like, three kids, and I would teach my son to play baseball, and go to football games on Sundays, and have barbecues with the whole neighborhood. I never imagined myself living outside the States," Joshua said.

"Yeah, Mills's dream sounds *brilliant*. Sorry, mate. Yours is good, too. Hers is just way better," Lucas said.

Like I said before, I didn't stick around for every minute of their lives. I didn't need to; I was just waiting for my happy ending that seemed to be taking forever to happen. I didn't stick around to see all of the filming of the second film. I didn't need to. It was a lot of late nights, a lot of laughs, a lot of intense scenes and a lot of excitement to be making such popular films.

All the while, Amelia wrote a new novel she was looking to publish, and all the while, she worked on her college assignments while practicing work in a field that had nothing to do with her major. It was hard. There was nothing easy about doing all that at once, but if anyone could do it, it was Amelia Alverson. At the end of filming of the second film, she was set to graduate from Stanford University, and the three first people she invited to her graduation were Eva Noble, Lucas Evans, and, of course, Joshua Clemons. They all three accepted eagerly and when the day for her graduation rolled around, the four of them found themselves in Palo Alto, California in nice outfits, driving to the graduation.

The university had asked Amelia to make a speech, since, in her short life, she had already done so very much. She had been able to keep everything quiet about her having written novels during the press tour. No one had asked about it because her pen name was different. But Stanford knew. It was one of the reasons they had asked her to come to their school. Most of the students didn't know, but she was terribly afraid that one of the faculty members was going to say something about it. She needed to tell the boys and she had chosen how she was going to do it: in her speech. She didn't want anyone to ruin the surprise. They would be in the front row and their reactions would be priceless.

"I'm offended that no one asked me to make a speech." Lucas leaned over Eva to whisper to Joshua. She elbowed him playfully.

"They probably were afraid of what you were going to say," she whispered, smiling.

Joshua grinned, about to comment himself, until he saw the President of the University come up to the podium and address the crowd. Joshua leaned back in his chair, as did Lucas. Today was about Amelia and they knew it. Lucas smiled at her on the stage in her cap and gown. He was the very picture of the older brother she had never had. Joshua looked at her, smiling even though she couldn't see him. She looked so beautiful, so happy, and he loved her so much.

"And now over to Amelia Alverson," said the current speaker. Neither of the boys had listened to or bothered to find out the identity of the speaker.

Amelia stood up and walked to the podium to applause. The boys took out their cameras.

"I could stand up here today and tell you that having this degree will make your lives so much easier, that a piece of paper will make your whole life worthwhile. If I did say that, then I would be abiding by every rule ever established in a graduation speech. I don't want to do that. The difference that this paper makes to your life isn't that it makes you a better person. It might make you more money, but it won't make you a better person. What makes you a better person is what you do with this degree—if you use it to help someone, find a cure for a disease, build a bridge sturdier and more durable then it would have been. Do some good in the world. Write a novel that changes people's lives, makes them think differently. Do what you love and you will make others happy around you. Because, my fellow graduates, life is like a novel. There is a beginning, a middle, and an end—" she looked at her two best friends. This was where she was supposed to tell them, but she couldn't, not here, not in front of everyone. "Actually, scratch all that. Here's what you really need to know.

"My whole life, I thought success was in how much money you make, or the kind of house you have, but that's not true. None of that is. Success isn't measured in dollars; success is measured in smiles. I know that probably sounds lame, and cheesy, but listen—" she turned to face the students and no longer the crowd. "You can spend your life trying to get rich, and that's great. You now have loads of money. The only difference is that now you don't have time. You used up your time trying to get all this money that really isn't going to do you any good where you're going." She turned back to the crowd. "I'm not saying never work and have no money to where you can't eat. I'm saying that instead of looking for the top paying job, look for the job that does what you like. Make friends, have dinner parties, tell jokes, make someone else happy.

"I've had people tell me that writing a novel sounds awful and that I couldn't pay them to do it. They've never understood why I would waste my time doing it. Sometimes *I* don't understand why I waste my time doing it. But then I come up with an incredible scene where I feel like everything just falls into place and I've never been happier. I never wrote because I thought I would get rich

doing it. I write because I know that writing is the only thing that helps me clear my head. That's what I want everyone here today to find, the one thing that clears your head, and I want you to take five minutes, if you can't find a way to turn it into a job, just five minutes, to do that every day. It may seem useless to everyone else, but if it makes you happy, then do it. Life is short, too short to do a job you hate with a boss you hate. That's what I want everyone here to remember: you have a piece of paper that opens doors, so use it to open the right ones. Thank you."

"Did she just improvise most of that speech?" Lucas whispered to Eva as they both stood up clapping with the rest of the crowd.

"She did, and it was the best speech I've ever heard,"

Eva said, smiling as she clapped louder.

"Did we just find out she's a writer?" Joshua asked, leaning over to Eva and Lucas as everyone continued to applaud.

"Did you two seriously never look at the author page in the back of the *Aliens* books?" Eva asked. "She wrote the whole series while she was in high school. She's written like six books to date and is in the middle of another one. She has a website."

"Of course we knew that, he was only kidding," Lucas said, leaning behind Eva and mouthing at Joshua, *"Did you know that?"*

Joshua shook his head and they both turned their attention back to Amelia as she returned to her seat.

Three days later, under the California sunset on the Golden Gate Bridge, Lucas Evans proposed to Eva Noble.

CHAPTER TEN
INTERVIEWS

Amelia didn't like the red carpet events of a movie. What she did like was the promotional tour. She loved the questions, thinking, hanging out with Joshua and Lucas, being on the road, and seeing new places. She loved it. However, it was a lot of pressure, especially on her because she was the star. The production team selected the three of them for interviews, press conferences, everything, changing the backdrop of other actors who would accompany them.

"Ams, are you okay?" Joshua asked. She was standing on the balcony at his house in L.A. She, Lucas, and Eva had been playing board games downstairs when she had excused herself to go to the restroom and never come back. The tour was in full swing and with interviews almost the whole day, it was rare she got a moment to herself.

"This probably sounds stupid, Josh, but it's a lot. It's all too much," she said, turning to him with her large green eyes. "Writing novels, making movies, writing more novels, making more movies, never being able to make mistakes because you're a role model for kids and you can't let them down."

"Ams, no one expects you to be perfect," Joshua said, putting his hand on the small of her back as she looked at him.

"Yes, they do. They have my whole life. I just feel it so much more now. It hurts, their pressure," she said. Her green eyes searched his for the same pressure.

"Ams, you've written so many books, you can stop," he said, gently. "Don't keep doing it if it drives you insane."

"I know, I know, my parents say the same thing, but I can't. None of you understand the pain of an untold story inside you. If I don't write these stories, then no one will and then—then they die with me and that hurts worse than anything else. Sometimes I hate writing, I hate it so much, but I'm not done, I'm never done. I can't stop because I'm not *done*," she said, looking down at the pool.

It was then that Joshua realized he had fallen in love with the tortured soul of an artist, someone who saw the world differently then he ever would. She expected perfection of herself when perfection wasn't possible, even for her.

"You don't have to work so hard to be perfect," he said. Joshua himself had never worked towards perfection. He had only worked towards his own happiness. It was a luxury Amelia had never had. He saw the frustration in her eyes because he didn't understand, then he saw her smooth it away. She was used to people not understanding. He wanted to, he wanted to understand more than he had ever wanted anything in his whole life. He just couldn't. He didn't understand how something that drove you mad could also be your salvation.

"I wanted my idols to be perfect," she said quietly. "I expected them to be."

"That's because you expect perfection of yourself and nothing less of everyone around you," he said gently.

"I suppose that's a horrible trait to have."

"No, it's one of the best."

She pulled away from him. Walking toward the other side of the terrace, she threw up her arms in frustration. "I just don't know how to make the voices in my head stop. All these characters, they're always there, *always*. Sometimes it's good, they help me, but they're always talking to me, giving me new ideas. I want so badly for them to leave me alone so that I'm done. But they won't."

"Ams—" Joshua started to say.

Her expression of pure frustration and pain smoothed over. The anger in her eyes quenched itself, or, more likely, was subdued by her powerful personality. She was used to this then, the madness inside.

"I'm sorry. It's very unfair of me to dump all of this on you. It's not your problem, it's mine. I will solve it on my own without bothering other people. Please forget I said anything."

With that, she nodded curtly to him and walked past Lucas, who had come up to check on them. She went downstairs to continue the board game with Eva. Lucas had heard the whole thing.

"She's never told anyone that."

"What?" Joshua asked, distracted by what he had just heard.

"You could just see it in her eyes, in the way she formed the words. She's never said them out loud," Lucas said, walking out onto the terrace to join his best friend.

"I didn't know what to say. I don't know what that's like, to never be done with anything, your mind never at rest," he replied, shaking his head after her.

"She wouldn't want it any other way. It drives her mad at times. I watch the fissures appear in her mask, but have you ever seen her write? I have, on set sometimes, when it's not her turn and she's waiting around. She doesn't read or goof off like most. She chooses to write. Have you ever seen her then?"

"No."

"You've never seen her until you've seen her write

or talk about what she's written. When she writes, her face is a mask. The perfect words flow from her fingers onto the keyboard effortlessly, never lacking the correct word. But when she reads it out loud, it's incredible. Her eyes light up. They sparkle like the ocean under the sun. Her whole complexion lights up. She's beautiful because in that moment she knows exactly who she is and where she belongs. Writing may give her demons, but it also gets rid of a lot of them," Lucas said, looking after her, as if he could see her writing.

"Her books are incredible," Joshua commented.

"Of course they are. She's wanted to be a writer since she was a small child. It's all she's ever practiced. She did what her parents wanted, the math, the studying, but all she ever wanted to do was write. Watch her when she hasn't written. She looks impatient. She seems almost trapped in that head of hers. Her cage is only opened when her keyboard is. It will drive her insane, but it will also keep her sane. She loves to be doing twelve different things at once. Sometimes it seems like it's a bit much, but then she has nothing to do and she's bored out of her very mind. Her imagination is what keeps her going. It entertains her when nothing else does. In that respect she is like a child," Lucas said, smiling slightly.

"How do you know this stuff?" Joshua asked, shocked.

"You see her on the outside, you look at those green

eyes, but you never focus on what is in them because you are too busy dreaming about what you will put in them. She will never be yours, and you will never be hers, until you can learn to understand her. The madness and all."

"She never opens up to me, though," Joshua pointed out.

"Then give her a reason to. It's not hard to know when she's writing. She has her laptop out, her gaze is elsewhere, she may look up and see you but she isn't seeing you, she doesn't hear you. Watch her then and you will learn more about her than you ever could talking to her. She is much too secretive for that," Lucas said, smiling at just how secretive she was.

110

"Hey," Lucas said, pushing open the door to Joshua's bedroom.

Amelia looked up and smiled slightly. "Hey."

"Mills, you can't just run out like that, you'll scare Joshua," Lucas said, walking in and shutting the door behind him.

Joshua's room was simple. He didn't spend much time there, after all. His room contained a big, grey bed in the center, night stands on both sides, and a door to a closet shoved carelessly into the corner, probably like the clothes in the closet. Directly in front of the door leading into the room was a large, floor-to-ceiling window looking out on the pool and the deck outside. Amelia sat on the bed, looking out at that.

"I think I'll scare him more if I stay in there," she said, smiling sadly. "I shouldn't have said what I said."

"You shouldn't have told him the truth?" Lucas asked, coming down to sit next to her.

"No, I never should have told him the truth." She looked away from Lucas.

"Mills, he's one of your best friends. If you can't tell him, who can you tell?"

"I shouldn't have to tell anyone. I should be able to keep quiet, to deal with it on my own. There is no need to tell anyone, no need to heap that on someone," she said, quietly.

"You don't get it, do you? We *care*, we want to help you, to talk to you. You're our best friend. That's not going to change just because you actually bother to tell us how you feel. You can't be perfect, we know that," Lucas said, placing his hand under her chin and guiding her eyes back towards his.

"I know that." She tried to look away but he wouldn't let her. He wanted her to see the truth in his eyes.

"I don't think you do. You want to be perfect, but you aren't human if you're perfect. I don't know what you are, but you aren't human. I don't know why you think that you need to be perfect, why you're so bloody afraid to do anything to anyone, tell anyone anything. You won't even look at guys, *any* guys. Maybe you had your heart broken, maybe someone hurt you, but I don't think that it was bad enough to warrant this," Lucas said, letting go of her face and shaking his head.

"Nice change of subject. How long have you been dying to ask that question?" Amelia asked. There was no malice in her voice, though, just a kind of sadness that seemed older than time itself.

"Have you ever had sex? Have you even kissed a guy? Mills, you're one of my best friends and sometimes I feel like I don't know anything about you," Lucas said. His eyes seemed to bore through her.

Amelia stood up and walked to the window, unable to look at Lucas any longer. It was as if she were seeing a different scene than was there, a scene from a long, long time ago. "Yes. Yes, to both. It was a long time ago, though. I gave my virtue, the one thing I thought I would save for the man I loved forever, and—and I just gave it away." Her voice sounded bitter.

Lucas was silent, as unmoving as a statue. He knew without her having to say it, knew that these were words not to be repeated to Joshua. He respected that. Joshua would never know what he, Lucas, was about to hear unless Amelia chose to tell him herself.

"I loved him so much, more than I ever thought I could love anyone. He asked, and I, in my stupid innocence, thought that meant he loved me the way that I loved him. He didn't."

"Mills, that was a long time ago," Lucas said gently.

"It's a battle scar, one so deep though that instead of killing me instantly, instead of mercifully ending it, it's killing me from the inside out. I tried sewing it back up, but sometimes the blood slips out of the wound before I can clean it. I guess this is that blood," Amelia said with a bitter laugh. She was quiet for a long time before saying, "I'm not afraid of love, Luc. I guess I'm just afraid of what it will do to me when people use it."

Lucas walked up behind her and touched her arm gently. "I'm sorry, Mills. You deserve better, much better."

She looked up at him and smiled that sad smile that broke Lucas's heart. "The thing is: I don't."

New York Radio, *The Wolf*, 2030

"We thought we would make this interview fun by doing a little game. The object of the game is simple: I will ask a question about one of you and whoever gets it right first gets the point. Sound good to you three?"

"Absolutely."

"You two are going down."

"Please, Luc. You don't know what you're talking about."

"If Amelia got arrested, who would be the first she would call?"

"Bollocks! What kind of question is this?"

"Ams would never get arrested!"

"Okay, Amelia, who would Joshua call? Remember, we're testing how well you know each other."

"Me."

"You?"

"Me."

"Joshua?"

"Super accurate. She wouldn't yell at me, she would just solve the problem. Then she would help me find the right way to tell my mother because my mother loves her."

"Okay, next question: who would Amelia come to if she found out she was pregnant?"

Amelia laughed. "I would hope I would call my husband, the father!"

"Bollocks. She would call Eva."

"I agree with that. Ams?"

"Actually, now that I think about it, you guys are probably right. I would call Eva, Lucas's fiancé."

"Okay—"

"Wait! Can I ask a question of Mills?"

"Um, all right. Lucas?"

"Brilliant! Who was your first celebrity crush?"

Amelia laughed. "Oh gosh, this is super embarrassing. It's gone now, I don't have a crush on this person anymore—"

"Yeah, yeah, who?"

"Josh."

"Me?"

"Him?"

"Yeah, okay, most of my friends did, and I was like ten and he was thirteen so he was older, and I thought he was really sweet—"

"—but then you met him and realized he was a prat?"

Amelia laughed again. "No! I realized that he was in fact a sweet guy, but that was just a childhood crush! I don't even think it was a real crush! I was ten! It was just the first time I was like *I would let him hold my hand on the playground.* I haven't had a crush on him in years!"

"That's too bad. It would have been beautifully awkward on set. Are you sure you couldn't develop the crush again?"

"Never say never."

"Lucas, you totally lost."

"Not in life, I haven't."

"Too philosophical."

"Would you ever date a costar?"

"I mean never say never, but I don't know. I've never really wanted to date an actor. I would want someone super real. A lot of my closest friends are actors and I would want someone who wasn't from that world. Just to have to a change of scene, you know?"

"But then they would never really understand what you go through."

"True, they would never understand the insanity

of it, but maybe that's a good thing. I would finally have someone else who could say, *That's insane, I can't believe someone would do that.* Everyone here is so hard to shock. I guess I would want someone who is as easy to shock as I am. I mean, people following you for a picture? That's insane."

The worst part for Amelia was when the interviewer decided to get a little too personal and Amelia had to be a little too closed off.

"What's your dream guy?"

"Me, obviously."

"Shut up, Luc. My dream guy?"

"Yeah, like is he funny, is he sincere, is he romantic, is he smart, is he drop-dead gorgeous?"

"Well, um, I guess my dream guy is funny. He doesn't take things too seriously. I guess romantic would be nice? Nothing cheesy, though. I guess he would have to be able to think for himself." She laughed. "Good-looking is nice, but if he can't talk and we can't have fun, then it's not going to last!"

"Joshua, what about your dream girl?"

"How about me? No one ever asks about my dream girl!"

"Okay, Luky Luc, what's your dream girl?"

"Well actually it's a *who.* My dream girl is Eva."

"Lame."

"That's why no one asks you."

"Who did you want me to say? Rihanna?"

"No, they want a type."

"Eva."

"Whatever. Josh, *you* answer the question."

"Um, well I guess she has to be funny. Like Ams said, a sense of humor is important. Dating the next *it* girl isn't important. I would want a girl who's smart, not an airhead. They get very boring very fast. Someone who likes sports, and someone who wouldn't mind riding on the back of my motorcycle."

"For the millionth time, Josh, that isn't *safe*. You could *die*. I keep telling you. Maybe one of these days you'll listen to me."

"Maybe one of these days he will."

"Probably not today, though."

"No, probably not today."

"Joshua, I don't think she'll ever be yours, mate," Lucas said, walking into Joshua's living room and sitting down.

"I know. I'm beginning to think that, too," Joshua replied, looking up sadly from the Giants baseball game they had been about to watch.

"Why don't you move on? I love Amelia, nothing will ever change that, but I don't want to see you waste your whole life, years of happiness, on someone who won't let you make her happy."

"I don't want to do that, either," Joshua replied.

"Then don't. Move on," Lucas said, gently.

"I can't. Part of me wants to, wants to find someone else, but it's like a puzzle, when you find a piece that you just know goes in one spot but no matter how many times you try to force it in there it won't work. You keep trying, though, keep trying because you know in your heart that that piece goes there. You just don't know how to turn it to make it work. There are other pieces in the set, other pieces that might fit. There would be a bit of empty space, but overall an unimportant amount. But it looks wrong. The picture just doesn't seem to link up. So, you remember that old piece you found and try again, hoping against all hope that this time it will work. It doesn't, but you never give up. Someday, maybe in a long time, maybe tomorrow, you'll pick up the puzzle piece and see that you were being stupid. All you had to do was turn it and then it fits perfectly. Amelia is that puzzle piece. She's the missing piece. I know she fits, I just don't know how yet."

"Well I hope you can figure it out sooner rather than later, mate, before it's too late," Lucas said.

"Me too, man. Me too."

"Plus, I mean, in the mean time, at least I get to be best friends with her. Is there anything better than being best friends with your crush?" Joshua asked.

"I mean, dating your crush, probably."

CHAPTER ELEVEN
SECOND CHANCES

It had been three years since Amelia and Joshua had first laid eyes on each other, three years since he had fallen in love with her, three years since she had resisted falling in love with him. Three years, three *long* years for Joshua, three short years of friendship for Amelia. This isn't to say that Joshua hadn't had brief hookups, hookups that had all of Hollywood buzzing, but they never meant anything to him. They were an attempted distraction, but nothing distracted him long. Amelia was now twenty-four and Joshua and Lucas were both twenty-seven.

"Mate, I'm sorry to say it again, but maybe you should try going out with another girl. Mills will come around, I'm sure, but maybe you should ask another girl out. You know, try to make her jealous?" Lucas asked.

Joshua knew exactly who Lucas was talking about. There was a new girl in the cast, Melissa Morgan. She was very pretty, charming, a fantastic actress, and yet, to Joshua, she was the most annoying girl on the planet. He knew Lucas was right, though. He did need to at least attempt to move on. That wasn't what he said, though.

"She doesn't even *like* me."

"She's been checking you out since filming started, a month and a half ago," Lucas said, rolling his eyes. He knew exactly what Joshua was doing.

"But—"

"But nothing. You're asking her out. Worst case scenario: she drives you insane for one night, best case scenario: you marry her."

"Um..."

"Um... You know what I mean. Go ask her out."

He did. He asked the new girl out and she said yes. Three years hadn't changed the fact that Joshua was still very handsome and very popular with the ladies. Amelia was still supposed to be dating Michael, though they were set to break up soon. They were friends, but nothing more.

So Joshua went on this date with Melissa. Filming was in San Francisco and Los Angeles for this film, so he took her somewhere nice, near the Golden Gate Bridge, at night. It was very romantic, except he didn't care.

"So, this is your first movie, right?"

"Yes! It is! I can't believe you remembered!" she

exclaimed, beginning to prattle off about how much she loved acting and the film business.

Ams never would prattle on about this. She isn't anywhere near this annoying. If she were here, we would be laughing about when the Dodgers' pitcher walked the winning run home last night. Instead I'm stuck here with this really annoying girl. Maybe I should go visit Amelia after this tonight... Her parents' house is only about an hour outside of the city... They're away visiting her sister at Vanderbilt and her mother's family for the month...

"Don't you just *love* sunsets, Josh? I'm sorry, is it okay if I call you Josh? Amelia does and I like it so much more..."

No! "Sure, no problem. Sunsets are great..."

She prattled on like that all evening. Well, she didn't actually prattle on. She just seemed to prattle to Joshua because he really couldn't have cared less about what she said. All he could think about was what a major waste of time this was when he could be with Amelia, watching the Giants game instead of checking the updates on his phone. Finally, he just couldn't take it anymore.

"Melissa, this has been a really fun night, but I haven't learned all my lines for tomorrow, so I should probably get back to the hotel to do that."

"Oh, of course!"

He didn't even have a scene tomorrow, but then she didn't know that, and as a minor character, she didn't have one either. She wouldn't find out. He paid for dinner and took her home before driving to Pacifica to go see the end of the game with Amelia.

He drove up to the house and smiled. It looked like a castle. Not quite as large as a castle, but almost, and beautiful, chic, and well maintained. There were new flowers and trees along with some perfectly placed furniture outside. Amelia rarely spent time at home, so much were they all on the road. Joshua had never been here before but was glad of the chance, the chance to see the child she had been. He looked up towards the steps leading to the door.

Amelia was an absolute neat freak and loved to clean everything around her. No doubt by the time her parents got home the whole house would be spotless. He walked up to what he assumed was the front door, and, knowing Amelia as he did, looked around for a loose rock in the castle, pulled it out, and there lay the keys.

The doors were a stunning mahogany wood and I smiled, following him inside the beautiful entryway as he shut the door behind him. He locked the door behind him. He yelled her name. She didn't answer. Her car was out front. She hadn't heard him. I glided up the stairs and found her in the process of cleaning up the linen closet, wearing short shorts and a black sports bra. She was barefoot and her long blond hair was pulled back into a ponytail. Joshua wore nice black pants and a nice white shirt. I could hardly wait to see the contrast. I glided back down the stairs and whispered in his ear. He took off up the elegant circular staircase. The whole house looked like a castle on the inside, too—a castle with a very open floor plan.

He walked quietly up the hall, with his nice shoes not making a sound on the carpeted floors. The door to the linen closet was slightly ajar. He pushed it open and tried to keep his mouth from dropping. He had never seen Amy with her shirt off. It was a sight to see. Her stomach was muscular in all the right places, toned. She had a nasty scar on her back, but his eyes weren't drawn there. His eyes were drawn over the hard muscle that flexed as she lifted up a heavy bucket and slid it onto the shelves she had built. He knew why.

She turned to look at him. "Josh! I'm not wearing a shirt! Who let you?" She immediately covered up her stomach, or at least attempted to.

"Um... Ams... I know you. It wasn't hard to figure out where you would hide the key, somewhere clever," he said, forcing his eyes to focus on her face and not on her bare stomach. His eyes shifted to her back, to the long, thin scar that covered almost all of it. He now understood why he had never seen her in a backless dress.

"Ams, what happened to your back?" he asked, gently.

She looked at him, really looked at him—at the

123

concerned look in his eyes, at the furrowed brow as his brain attempted to come up with all of the reasons she might have that, and at his lips, slightly apart, the words having just tumbled out of his mouth. She could hide the truth from him, that's what I thought she would do. Instead, she bit her lip, and after a moment, began to talk. The words seemed to throw themselves out of her mouth, as if she couldn't speak quickly enough to tell him, to see the rejection in his eyes. Her scar had always made her imperfect in her mind, not quite whole.

He recognized that this was top-secret information and his heart leapt at being confided in but he also realized how painful doing this must be for her, so he tried to make a joke. "You know, you could always attach an axe to it and pour fake blood on it for Halloween."

She laughed. The tension eased from her shoulders. "I tried that once. The fake blood just ended up all over my pants. You don't think it's a problem, though?"

He looked at her gently. His mind searched for the right words for how he felt. "You underwent a back brace and pain and surgery and more pain. There's no need to be ashamed of that."

She smiled before changing the subject. "Did you lock the door behind you?"

"Of course."

Her arms relaxed. "Well, I guess you've seen me now, no use covering up. It's sweltering in here."

"Do you mind if I take my shirt off, too?" he asked, unsure where his sudden spike of confidence was coming from. "I agree, it's really hot in here."

She nodded. She wouldn't mind the view. "It's because of all this cloth and the buckets. My mother had thrown *everything* in here. You couldn't see the floor." They could see most of it now.

He unbuttoned his shirt, trying to hide the shake in his hands. She turned back to her work. He finally got it off and folded it neatly like he knew she liked and set it on a nearby shelf.

"Well, it looks great now," he said. It did, too. You could see most of the black wooded floors. The shelves were neatly organized.

"Thank you. Weren't you supposed to be on a date with Melissa?" she asked, folding some cloth and placing it on the shelf. Her voice was careless, what he should have recognized as guarded, but he was too busy thinking about how hot it was and how much he would like to kiss her.

"Uh... Yeah, yeah I was, but I took her home." He attempted to calm his voice to make it sound normal.

"Why?"

"Because there wasn't anything there," he replied, reaching over her shoulder to fold something.

"Josh, you've only been on one date since I've known you. You can't expect to go on one date and expect to meet the one," she said, rolling her eyes, not to be undone by the proximity of his skin.

"I know. I guess that when I meet her, I'll just know," he said. He did know, she just didn't. "And what about you? You haven't exactly been on many dates, either."

"True, but, through no fault of my own. I've been tied up to Michael for two and a half years," she said. The harder she had pushed the publicists to let her break off the relationship, the more they resisted. It was making the fans go crazy, they said. They were even more into the movie. They weren't wrong.

Her eyes avoided the tattoos on his lower body and the way his muscles gleamed in the light. She could still see them, though, the way his muscles flexed and released every time he moved, the way his tattoo seemed to move perfectly in sync with his every movement, almost making it look graceful. There was nothing more in this world that she wanted than to trace that tattoo, to feel his skin beneath her fingers, moving and flexing to her touch. Not that she was looking.

"I guess you have a point. What are you going to do when you two *break up?*" Joshua asked.

He was attempting to carefully avoid looking at everything. He had seen her in a swimsuit, but that had been a one-piece. This was different, very different. There was so much more skin here, so much more was revealed. Her shorts fit her in all the right places and finished just below the butt. They revealed a lot, the whole outfit revealed a lot, but not enough. There was too much space between them, too much clothing between them. Her hair was in that ponytail and it was driving him crazy. He wanted nothing more than to rip off the ponytail holder, to let her silky blond hair flood down her back and through his fingers as he pulled her close, shutting off any remaining distance between them. His heart was pounding. He had never wanted anything more, and yet, using the largest amount of self-restraint I had ever seen, he didn't do anything. He just stood there and stared at her. It didn't cost him nothing to do, though. His teeth bit down so hard on his lip that it began to bleed. Amelia didn't notice. She wasn't looking.

She laughed. "I don't know. Be careful, I guess."

She reached over to pick up a bucket. He tapped her hand and she moved it, surprised at his touch, as he lifted the bucket and put it exactly where she would have placed it. "Why be careful?"

"I could have picked that up, you know," she said, wrinkling her nose. "Wait, Josh, your lip is bleeding!"

She reached her finger up gently and brushed the blood off from his puncture wound. Her fingers were so delicate as they came into contact with his lips. He wanted to kiss each one of them but he couldn't.

"I know. Now, why be careful?" He smiled. He thought it was cute when she wrinkled her nose.

"Because, I know myself well enough to know that once I give my heart to someone, I give everything I have to someone. That results in a lot of pain. Or at least it did for me the only time I did it," she said. Her green eyes seemingly looked back on a time when that broken heart had changed her life.

"But it's good, getting your heart broken. It's a part of life," he said, wanting to bring her back to him, away from that time.

"It almost destroyed me. I have to be very, very careful in the future not to let that happen again," she said.

"Well, Luc and I will make sure that doesn't happen," Joshua said. He wanted to ask what had happened, who had broken her heart, but he knew better than to ask. Amelia told the bare minimum of what needed to be told— no more, no less.

"I don't know that you will be able to. Logic doesn't come into it, unfortunately," she said, smiling sadly.

He had been putting something on the shelf to the side of her. She turned in his arms, to face him, which she hadn't been doing. They were face to face, their scents mixing with each other. I thought for sure he would kiss her. I thought for sure she would kiss him. The sexual tension was palpable.

"Logic doesn't come into it when I'm in love, either," he murmured.

128

The lights went out. She pulled away. "Another power outage, third one this week. The struggle that is living out in the middle of nowhere and your parents refusing to purchase a generator despite the fact that this happens so often."

"What should we do?" he asked, closing his eyes in utter pain, though she couldn't see them.

"We should order pizza and get flashlights," she said, grabbing his hand and pulling him out the door of the linen closet and down the stairs to the kitchen where her cellphone was. "What time did you want to go home?"

"And leave you here in the dark? Do you have an extra bedroom?" he asked, smiling. He could still turn this around.

"I do, in fact. Are you sure you want to stay, though? It's a long drive back to the set." She tried to hide the smile in her voice, her happiness at his offer to stay, to not leave her alone in the dark.

"I don't have a scene tomorrow. Do you?"

She didn't. She grinned at him through the dark. "Pepperoni or cheese?"

He grinned back. It wasn't what he had wanted, what he had dreamt of, had this situation ever aroused, but it was much better than nothing.

They ended up going for pepperoni.

"Josh? Where are you?" Amelia called. They had lost each other going downstairs in an attempt to touch everything in the kitchen in order to find the flashlights.

"Over here! I think I found them—" Joshua said before a light turned on and Amelia found herself looking at Joshua through the glare of a flashlight.

"I'll say," she replied with a laugh.

"Got any mirrors? We can project this off one and shine it outside so that ships can see the coast," Joshua suggested.

"Or think that a chorus of angels is about to pop out and announce the second coming of the Messiah," Amelia said with a grin.

"Either way, fun for us."

CHAPTER TWELVE
HAPPY ENDINGS

Filming went well. The movie finished on time and the cast was dismissed. This left a month before the promotional tour was set to begin, a month between filming and a packed tour—a month in which Lucas Evans and Eva Noble got married in Paris. They got married in a church. Eva was Jewish, Lucas was Catholic. They had a large wedding in the church and a small ceremony in her synagogue. They were to be married by a priest, in robes, with the church filled with their friends.

It was a whirlwind event, a large wedding by all accounts. Joshua was, of course, the best man, while Amelia was the Maid of Honor. The two took their roles very seriously, helping the couple make all the decisions to ensure that everything would go smoothly.

Her phone rang. "Ams?"

"Josh, *stop* calling me. I'm in the middle of pinning something on Eva's dress. She has to be ready any minute."

"Okay, but Luc needs to know where you put his tie."

"Around his neck."

"*Ams.*"

"Dresser, top drawer to the left."

Silence.

"Got it, thank you, you're a lifesaver."

"Give me the damn thing."

A scuffle.

"Mills?"

"Luc, what do you want? Put on the tie and get ready. Eva is almost ready to walk down that aisle. You'd better be there when she does."

"Amelia Alverson, where the hell is the liquor?"

"Down the drain. I'm too smart for you."

"Bless you. I'm ready. What do I do? How does she look? Gorgeous? Can you take a picture without letting her know? Actually no, I'll just see for myself." More scuffling. "So sorry, see you in a moment. Joshua is attempting to reclaim his phone."

"Sorry, Ams. Ready to go?"

"Let's do this."

The ceremony was beautiful. Eva was stunning, Lucas was handsome. None of that was what took Joshua's breath away, happy as he was for his friend. Nothing had happened between him and Amelia that night the power had gone out at her house. They had both wanted something to happen, but they had both held back from letting it for fear of rejection. They had watched a movie on her laptop, eaten the pizza they had ordered, and then gone to sleep. In the morning, the power had come back on. She had made pancakes and he had made fruit smoothies after she showed him how to use a blender. It had been a painful snapshot in time, reminding him what his life could be like if they actually dated and one day got married.

Since she was the Maid of Honor and he the Best Man, it was his job to walk her down the aisle. All the while he was trying not to be blown away by how she looked in that light blue dress, and wondering what she would look like in white with him in black. He wondered if they would ever have those fun pancake mornings to themselves.

He couldn't help but remember walking into her childhood room while she was downstairs, and looking at the pictures on the wall of her and her friends. He had met most of them, but that wasn't what had struck him. What had struck him was her expression in each one of them. She looked happy, so carelessly happy. He had only ever seen her that happy a couple times, with that genuine smile that showed that she really enjoyed the people that she was with.

133

She hadn't spent much time here since going off to college, he knew that. He was still hurt to see that his photo wasn't there. She had always said that she wanted her old room just as it had been when she had left, a sort of snapshot in time. His photo belonged in her new home, not here. Her room had been full of books, full of books that he had never read but now wanted to. He wanted to read anything that would remind him of her, that would smell like her. He remembered her coming in as he looked at her walls of photos and she put her hand on the small of his back and smiled up at him.

"You and Luc should be up there too, you know. I just don't want to change anything, to disturb it. I love being able to come in here and remember the person I was when I left it like this. I vacuumed it and dusted it, but I don't want to move anything. It's like entering a time capsule. I come in here and I'm her again, that girl who wanted her books published so bad but wasn't sure what to do without a pen in her hand. I'm still her, I'm just published now." She bit her lip and added after a moment, "And I guess I'm in movies and stuff."

With those words, when he looked around, he saw something else. He saw the girl from those pictures, writing, always writing. Putting up these photos, laughing with her friends, doing homework, dreaming big, knowing who she was from a young age.

"You must have been a hell of a kid," he remarked,

134

smiling as he looked around at the photos, the MUN badges, the science fair medals, the Lego constructions, her swim team ribbons, her awards for community service. Everything was perfectly organized. It wasn't displayed, either. Things were placed carelessly, though they looked good, on a desk because before she'd moved she hadn't put them away. Ribbons were just sitting on a side table, as if she didn't know where to put them.

"I did a lot, that was for sure. I liked doing it all, though. I was bored if I wasn't doing everything I liked, and I liked a lot of diverse things. I wanted to do all of it. I was lucky, I could," she said, smiling.

"How do you deal with the rest of us? We must seem so dull to you," he said, smiling at her.

She laughed. "You're not boring! You're fascinating, I love trying to figure out what you will do next, what you're thinking, what your expressions mean. You laugh at all my jokes, which I appreciate. My dad was the only one who got them before."

He grinned. "That's because most of them require a lot of thinking and a degree in nuclear physics to understand."

"It's not *my* fault those are the funny ones!" she exclaimed, though she was laughing too. She had that real smile in her eyes, that smile she had in the photographs on the wall.

She had that smile now as they walked arm in arm

down the aisle, ahead of Lucas and Eva. She smiled at Lucas, proudly almost, like he was her little boy and she was marveling at how fast he had grown up. She seemed to delight in the whole wedding, being surrounded by people, doing everything to make Lucas and Eva happy. Joshua had never seen someone love to make others happy so very much. I smiled. Amelia may seem cold-hearted to you, dear reader, but that wasn't the problem. The problem was that her heart was too big and that her brain controlled it.

She looked up at Joshua and smiled, the smile reaching her eyes, filling their green with pure joy. She looked so excited, so happy. Dear reader, that was when Joshua knew, more than any other moment, that he wanted to walk her down an aisle again, when she was wearing white, and he wanted to see that same look in those green eyes. He would, too. He would just have to be patient. It would be a little while. Of course, looking back, I suppose even I was unsure as to how long.

Looking up at Josh, Amelia remembered Jamie, when he had come to her trailer on the last day of filming. She had been in the midst of cleaning everything and boxing it up.

"Joshua is in love with you, you know."

"No, he isn't. I really wish you would stop saying that," she said, picking up a photo of the two of them and putting it in a box. She glanced at the picture. They were both laughing together. Lucas had taken it during their stay in Paris. It was cold outside, that much was discernible from their coats and scarves, but that didn't stop them from being doubled over laughing over some long-forgotten joke. They both looked so happy, like there wasn't a care in the world. There was no way someone like that, some amazingly good guy, was in love with her.

"He is, and you are in love with him. Someday you two will realize that and you will date. And then, just like every movie star ever, you will have children and get old and ugly, and he will throw you over and find a new plaything. He only wants you because he thinks you don't want him. Remember that." With that, he'd left.

I remember watching her sit down on the bed. It was everything she had always thought about me, about love. She figured it wasn't permanent—that eventually I would fade from her life and go on to someone else's. She was very sadistic about such things. She had seen her parents argue, fight, fall out. They weren't divorced, they did love each other, but she didn't understand how you could fight and then just *make up*. When she felt an emotion, she felt it with all of her heart.

With everything she had, she felt doubt. She had never understood why anyone would love her. She looked at herself and she saw only the flaws. That was her problem. She had so many strengths, so many, but no one had ever told her about them. Much like with every other aspect of her life, people assumed that she was confident and happy. Why wouldn't she be? She seemingly had everything. No one thought she needed compliments. They didn't know she needed them with every fiber of her being. It was more than that, though. She needed to hear the compliments and understand that they were true, know in her heart of hearts that people weren't lying. She seemed to be the most secure person on the planet, but like I said, she was an incredible actress.

That's why, when Joshua looked at her as they walked down that aisle, he saw only happiness. She was happy, for Lucas and Eva, but she didn't know where her life was going. She had her career, but she feared most being alone. She could always write. That didn't matter. She just feared having no one to talk to when she was older, no one to make her smile. I would have given her an Oscar for her performance of confident young woman. Everyone else would have, too, if only they knew it was an act.

She did know one thing, though: that she was completely and totally in love with Joshua. She wasn't sure when this had happened or how. She thought she had been so careful. It could have been when they had pranked Jamie, it could have been when they worked late at night together on a scene, it could have been in the linen closet at her house, when he told her that her scar was like a battle scar. She didn't know. She wasn't sure she wanted

138

to. She wouldn't admit her feelings, though, not out loud. It would seem as if she were confirming it, sealing her fate, sealing the inevitable heartbreak that she saw in her future. And yet every moment without him felt like an eternity. She would do anything to see his smile. I smiled. I only wished he knew that, that his time had finally come. But he didn't.

They got to the end of the aisle, and, due to custom, they parted—both wishing they didn't have to, both unable to voice this wish.

"Now, Lucas, you just got married, correct?"

"About a month ago, yes."

"How was that? We have a photo."

"It was brilliant, as you, well as you can see. Eva, my wife, looked amazing. The service was lovely, the dinner after even better. We wanted to get married in between filming and the tour and it just seemed like the right time to do it."

"She does look great. You two got married in Paris, correct?"

"We did. It was very romantic. It was perfect placement because my family was close in England and most of her family had always wanted to come to Paris. It all worked out perfectly."

"But—you don't speak French, do you?"

Lucas laughed. "No! Well, a little, a very little. No,

Amelia was Eva's Maid of Honor—Amelia Alverson—and she speaks fluent French. They worship her in France for it. She got everything done that needed to be done with the locals."

"Were any other of your actor friends in your wedding?"

"Well Joshua, Joshua Clemons. He was my best man."

"Was he?"

There was applause.

"Well, I wasn't going to have some random bloke do it! It was a little too important for that!" Lucas said, laughing.

Amelia and Joshua were backstage, smiling, proud of their best friend as they looked on. Lucas glanced over at them briefly and smiled. He smiled that same smile that had brought them together that day they had decided to watch *Star Wars*, that smile that reminded them of their time in Paris and in London and just everywhere they had been together.

I had seen many different types of myself, felt many kinds of myself, but in that moment, in that moment where there was only them, I felt the rest of the world fall away. I felt them and their smiles. Time seemed to stop— they didn't need it anyway. It was infinite for them who controlled it, flowing and constantly changing. They didn't need it. They didn't need anyone, just each other. They were there for each other. They had been through a lot. Their friendship had been tested by distance, by time, by everything the universe could throw at them. Seeing their smiles that day, the way they seemed to communicate without words, I saw that they had really and truly won. The universe bowed to them and their friendship. I bowed to them and their love of themselves. They would be tested in the future, these bonds they had forged. The type of bonds would change, but, for better or for worse, Amy and Joshua were locked together and in it for the long haul. I heard their laughs in my ears. They knew it and it elated them.

CHAPTER THIRTEEN
RURAL AMERICA

The actors had two weeks after the promotional tour before filming for the last two movies, since they were a "Part I" and "Part II," as the last book was divided into two parts. The three, along with Eva, debated at length where they wanted to spend these two weeks. It was never debated who would be going. They knew it would be each other. Finally, with the promise of barbecue, they all agreed to go to visit Joshua's family in Tennessee. His family owned a nice farm with lots of space and acreage. It was summer and it would be hot. Not only hot, it would be miserably humid. They knew that. Amelia didn't mind the heat, nor did Joshua. Lucas, true to his English roots, despised great heat. Eva didn't care either way. It was three against one, therefore. Lucas was forced into going and he *wasn't* happy about it.

"Guys, it's *hot*. Actually worse, it's *humid*. Why in the world would you *pay* to go somewhere *humid*?"

"Because we have family here," Joshua replied, rolling his eyes. He was used to it at this point.

"*Why* would your family live here?"

"I don't know, you can ask them."

"I will. Maybe I can get them to move somewhere sensible, like in the UK, none of this *rural America* stuff," Lucas affirmed.

He didn't.

Joshua's parents were very sensible, kind people. They had lived all their lives in Tennessee and weren't planning on moving. Their farm was a lovely, almost modern thing, with lots of space to run around, with a lake behind it. Lucas and Eva had their own room, and Joshua and Amelia each did, too.

They had hardly deposited their bags in their respective rooms when Joshua's younger brother, David— who, incidentally, was a year younger than Amelia, and four years younger than his brother—dragged them all outside to go swimming in the lake.

Lucas, not to be outdone by the southern sun and humidity, lathered on the sunscreen as Joshua and Amelia laughed at him. He got the last word, though. Eva let him put sunscreen on her. He stuck his tongue out his friends and they laughed some more. Amelia and Joshua didn't bother with sunscreen, not because they thought they wouldn't get sunburnt, but because they didn't care. They were in the water from the moment they opened the back door.

Amelia wore her one-piece black swimsuit. Joshua wore navy blue swim trunks with his shirt off, revealing his tattoos. Luc wore red trunks, and Eva wore a blue and white striped two-piece. David resembled Joshua, but his features were more elf-like than his older brother's. He wore green swim trunks on this occasion. They looked like the movie stars that they were but acted like the children they had never gotten to be, running around, squirting water guns at each other, jumping into the water, laughing so hard that time-outs had to be called.

Soon they were all covered in mud from the surrounding lake. Their hair was wet, and none of them bothered to clean the mud off of their faces. Finally, it all ended as I had predicted: they teamed up and threw mud at each other in the place of snowballs, covering themselves in the slimy stuff, not even caring. Joshua's mother took a photo that day, a photo that currently hangs in Joshua and Amelia's house in London. The five of them are covered in mud, their hair dripping with it, their teeth a bright, blinding white against the wet soil that surrounded them. They were all holding onto each other, trying to get the other one muddier than they were and succeeding in getting themselves muddier too.

I smile, placing the photo down on their table. They're in the kitchen. They don't see me. No matter. I'm not up to this part of the story yet. I will be soon, though, so patience, dear reader.

Where was I? Ah, yes, that fateful summer which brought them even closer. They played in the mud, rendering themselves filthy, until they cleaned themselves before dinner so that they would be presentable to eat with the family.

Amelia chose to wear a summer dress, which was white with red flowers, banded at the waist, and loose everywhere else. The dress was modern with a touch of classic, matched with tan sandals. Joshua's mother, Jessica, who loved fashion, would love it. Eva also wore a summer dress. It was light green, skater style, tight at the top and loose at the bottom, also matched with sandals. Lucas and Joshua both wore tan shorts and polo shirts. It wasn't that dinner with the Clemons was necessarily a *nice* event, it was just a family event, and for Amelia and Eva who had only met the Clemons at one or two of the premiers, it was even more important to impress them. They wanted Joshua to be proud of his friends. Lucas had met them a few more times, but not too many more. None of them had ever stayed there before.

"Now Amelia, Joshua says that you love to write," Jessica Clemons said, passing Eva the salad. Jessica Clemons had short, bobbed blond hair. She was tan

146

and relatively attractive. She was also very protective of her sons, especially when it came to girls, romantic relationship or not.

The dining room was beautiful, redone recently, with a very open concept much like the whole house, with a grand archway leading into the kitchen, and another leading into the living room. The table was long, mahogany, and easily fitting the seven people that it held. It folded down for when it was just the family. That night, with Eva and Amelia's help, Jessica had prepared chicken parmesan. The boys would be in charge of the next meal. There was a seating chart: Amelia sat next to Joshua at the head of the table, much to her extreme discomfort. Joshua was to her right. His brother, David, was to her left. Joshua's mother claimed the other head. The girls had cooked, meaning they got the head places. Jessica's husband sat in between her and his second son, with Lucas and Eva across the table.

Amelia blushed at the mention of her writing. Joshua reached under the table and squeezed her hand. She glanced at him and he smiled. She smiled back.

"Yes, I do. I've known since I was a child that I wanted to be a writer. I just needed to grow up enough to actually write."

"You've written the series you three all act in the movies for, yes?" Joshua's father, John, asked. He looked like an older version of Joshua, distinguished, with a

147

few gray hairs in his tousled brown hair, altogether very handsome.

"Yes, sir," Amelia acknowledged.

"And you speak several different languages?" Jessica pressed. So that was their play: interview Amelia since this would be their first real relationship. They knew that their son was in love with her. It wasn't hard to tell. They also knew she wasn't in love with him, or so they thought. They wanted to know why.

Joshua didn't let go of Amelia's hand under the table. She was glad for it. She needed the comfort. Being given the third degree by your best friend's parents as they attempted to decide whether or not you were good enough for their child was abysmal at best.

"Yes: Italian, French, Mandarin, German, and, obviously, English. I learned most of them in school. My strongest language is probably French. A lot of my friends are French, which gives me a chance to practice often, and it was the one I started the earliest," she said, nodding. If she was nervous—which, incidentally, she was—no one but Joshua knew. He could sense it. He was the first person to ever sense the nerves under her perfect acting mask. Lucas didn't even notice. He thought Amelia never got nervous, and that this was a new thing, not something he would be prepared for.

"We wanted to start Joshua in languages when he was younger but none of the schools around here were good enough. David has taught himself some, haven't you?" his mother asked, looking at him. David barely heard her, though. His eyes were glued to Amelia.

David was a very smart boy. He loved math and science, had won every science fair he had ever entered, and was currently a senior at MIT in nuclear physics. He recognized the same brain in Amelia and he was determined to take advantage of it. His parents, while very nice and smart in their own way, never understood what it was he was doing. Joshua wasn't much better. Amelia had never minded Joshua's lack of understanding academically, maybe because she valued a good heart over a good head.

"You have a degree in mechanical engineering from Stanford, correct?" he asked of Amelia. With that, they were off to the races, discussing everything they had both learned in their studies, comparing experiments, basically having a grand time. Lucas and Eva didn't say a word all evening, but then this wasn't a problem for them. They were more than happy to let Amelia impress everyone. Also, neither they nor their other table companions knew a thing about what was being discussed and, rather than embarrass themselves, they chose the time-tested tactic of silence. It was awfully effective.

After dinner, Amelia and Joshua joined Josh's father in watching the college football game. Amelia didn't love American football, but she didn't hate it, either.

Growing up in a sports family had taught her a lot. She knew all of the players, all of the plays, and was generally a great fan to watch with, never getting too worked up but getting worked up enough. Joshua's father thought she was brilliant. That was two members of the family she had won over. Now she just needed to win over his mother. She wasn't even doing it on purpose; she was doing it naturally. She wasn't trying to win them over, not really. She was just trying to be nice to them because they mattered to Joshua, which now meant that they mattered to her. Funny how I work like that, sometimes.

That night, when she had finally retired to her room to sleep, and Joshua got up to retire in turn, his father stopped him. "Don't let her get away. She is the perfect woman: smart, charming, pretty, funny, loves sports. What more could you want? Don't let her get away."

Joshua had felt like screaming that he was trying but instead all he said was, "I won't."

That night, Amelia, Eva, and Lucas were invited to an event of Joshua's the next day. He didn't tell them what it was. He just asked them to come. When they awoke, he was no longer at the house. His parents weren't, either.

"Guys, what do we do? Where does he have us going.? We should be dressed appropriately for whatever it is," Lucas said.

"He has us going to a graduation," Amelia said, bewildered, holding up the paper she had received with the address.

"How do you know that?" Eva asked.

"I looked up the address. It's a football stadium. I clicked on the events for the day. An online college rented it out for their graduation," Amelia said, rolling her eyes that neither of her friends had thought to do that.

So, two hours later, the three of them showed up, wearing nice outfits. Lucas was in a suit, and Amelia wore a black dress, which was sleeveless, tight up top, and poufy on the bottom. Eva wore a body-tight pink dress ending just above her knees, with her hair curled.

Amelia insisted they needed to stop at the grocery store to get Joshua a wreath flower necklace. She picked a light blue one, her favorite color. The three then got in the car and drove to the football stadium.

"Did you lot know he was doing this?" Lucas asked. "I've noticed that I typically find out everything last, but don't tell me you two knew *this* and didn't tell me!"

"Nope," Amelia said.

"I had no idea," Eva said.

"I wonder why he did it, then, if he didn't want to tell us until now," Lucas said, not that he couldn't guess.

They didn't know.

They were seated with Joshua's parents when they arrived, around the center of the field. The stage was near the front. They all talked and waited until the graduates walked down the center aisle in their black robes with their black caps. Amelia saw Joshua and they locked eyes.

That was when she fell head over heels in love with him. It wasn't because she had found out he was a college man, and it wasn't because she thought he looked great in black robes. It was the look on his face, the look in his eyes. That look of pure pride. Not cruel, stuck-up pride, but a childish pride, the look that said *look at me, I did it*. He looked so very happy, so very proud of his accomplishment, that she found herself wondering how she could ever live without that look, the look that lit up her whole world.

The graduation took all of two hours. The diplomas were passed out, the speeches made. Joshua had been asked to speak, much like Amelia had, having as much to do with their celebrity as anything else.

"We all have our diplomas now—proof that we did this. Proof that we all went to college and graduated, proof that we—we who have had to take classes around our jobs and families, we who were up late writing essays, we who have worked so hard to be here today—we have proof that we worked hard to achieve this goal and we did. This wasn't easy for any of us. It was difficult and trying, but we are all wearing these robes today because we decided that this was where we wanted to be. We're here because of ourselves, no one else. That is something to be proud of. Thank you."

His speech wasn't quite as long as Amelia's, but it wasn't supposed to be. That wasn't the highlight of the graduation, either. The highlight was when the graduates were allowed to descend into the audience to their families. Joshua had selected the seating for his family, so he knew exactly where they were. He practically ran down the steps of the podium, with his robes flowing around him, straight to them. He wasn't running to his parents, though. He wasn't even running to Lucas. He was running to Amelia.

She opened her arms wide and, when he got there, threw them around his neck as he lifted her off the ground. Her heart was pounding against his.

"I did it, Ams, I did it," was all he could whisper in her ear.

"I'm so proud of you," she whispered back.

Lucas patted him on the back, saying that Joshua's father, brother, and Lucas himself were going to take the other girls home, seeing as the men needed to get started early with the preparation of the celebratory dinner. Really it was an excuse to leave them alone.

When they were gone, when everyone else was slowly vacating the football field, Joshua let go of Amelia to look at her, to properly look at her.

"Why did you do this, Josh?" she asked. "Is it because of what Jamie said?"

He shook his head. It was for her and for him, to prove to both of them that he was worthy. He couldn't say that, though. They weren't dating. She didn't like him, not like that, so instead he said, "I wanted to see if I could do it."

"Because David could?" she asked.

"No, because I wasn't sure I could," he replied. Deep down he wanted to prove to himself, and prove to her, that he was worthy of her love. This had been the way he had chosen to prove it.

She threw her arms around his neck again in a hug. "I always knew you could do whatever you put your mind to! Going to college around our work schedules, it's not easy."

"It's not Stanford," he mumbled in her ear.

"No, it's better now, because you went here and that makes it special," she replied, her voice tickling his ear.

"Kiss up," he replied, letting go of her.

She laughed and punched him lightly in the shoulder. "When did you become my best friend?"

He smiled. The words warmed his heart. "I really don't know. It just sort of happened."

"Like everything we do," she pointed out with a slight laugh.

"Exactly."

I knew how they became so close. The difference was, I had learned that with most great friendships, humans don't know how they happen. They just sort of *do*. Maybe that's what makes them so strong. One moment they aren't there, the next he or she can't imagine his or her life without the other. There's a beautiful aspect to it, really.

They still weren't dating, but this was a step in the right direction. I laughed silently as I watched them, so much closer from the starting point but not quite at the finish line. Part of me wanted them to speed up and finish the race. Part of me knew that the longer this run went on, the more fun the end would be.

She placed the flowers that had been waiting on her chair until now around his neck and took his photo. One of the other graduates saw them together and asked if they would like a photo. They agreed, happy at not being asked for autographs or mobbed for once. For once, people were giving them a moment to themselves, alone and happy.

That photo is framed in their house now, too.

155

"Hey."

"Hey," Amelia said, looking up at Joshua. She was seated on a little bench next to the lake that they had all played in earlier. The sun was beginning to set, but Amelia had badly wanted a bit of fresh air, some space to think.

"Why are you out here?" Joshua asked.

"I was just thinking. You know, when I was little I couldn't think without noise. I always needed to have music on, people talking, something. I didn't actually like having all of that going on, I just didn't like the silence that came without it. I loved practicing going somewhere else in my head, listening to all of the hustle and bustle and yet not listening to any of it. It was a point of pride that people could talk to me and I could be millions of miles away in a made-up universe, watching people who weren't real interact. It was hard, too, when I was a kid, because I could hear this conversation going on in the back of my head with people no one else could see and I could hear this conversation going on in front of me with people everyone could see. That was great, it was all good fun, and I think I was too young to figure out how to make those fictitious people stop talking, anyway. Sometimes I had a hard time remembering who was real and who wasn't," Amelia explained without looking at him. She smiled after a moment. "Most writers have writers' block. I've always

had the opposite problem: too many ideas and too little time. I just never knew how to use that time properly."

"What about now?" Joshua asked, quietly.

"Now I don't wonder if it would have been a better idea to listen to all of the pointless ramble before there was no more pointless ramble to hear," Amelia said, quietly.

"If you want someone to ramble, I can always give it a try. Heck, I can read a book, a really boring book if you want to hear someone saying nothing interesting," Joshua said with a smile.

Amelia laughed. "I'll keep that in mind."

"You realize you just told me about your writing and I didn't run a million miles away," Joshua said with a grin. He was pleased she was finally opening up to him.

She laughed again. "Congrats. You can clearly deal with the insanity that is me."

They were quiet a moment, staring out at the lake, hearing the crickets come out and begin to chirp as the sun continued its descent.

"So you always had these characters in your mind with complicated stories?" Joshua asked.

Amelia grinned as if she were looking at a scene playing out before her, a long forgotten memory.

"When I was a real little kid, like five or six, I used to play Barbies. I used to come up with these massively complicated games, with plot twists, deceit, love, friendship, and life lessons. I had them all in my head and the dolls were perfect for helping me to get them out, to perfect them until I liked them. I would ask my parents to come play with me and every time they would have to sit in front of me for an hour, no less, so that I could explain how the entire story was going to go down. Who needed to die, who needed to make the sacrifices, everything. My mom always had to leave after that hour. She had other things to do and it was a lot to remember anyway. My dad would try to play with me but he would forget his character's development and the arc would be wrong and I would get frustrated and so I had to stop that. I had just started learning how to write and so I decided that maybe paper could listen to these stories and not get the arcs wrong or have other things to do. I decided that if I wrote those stories down, then I could change them, edit them. When I was about ten, the main characters in my *Aliens* series started to appear in the back of my head and there was no going back from there," Amelia said. Her eyes were distant but somehow familiar to Joshua.

"That's insane," Joshua said, smiling so that she knew he meant in a good way.

"Sometimes I wondered if I was insane. Most little kids don't have super long complicated stories going on in the back of their heads while they attend kindergarten. I think the only reason I managed to not go insane is because I knew, no matter how much better the universe in the back of my mind was, it only existed in the back of my mind."

"That had to be hard to accept as a little kid."

"What, that I wasn't the hero? That I had homework instead of a city to save?" Amelia laughed. "Yeah, sometimes it was, but it was also the best because if I wanted to be the hero, then I could be and then I could go back to the regular world and be a regular kid with no one looking to me to save the world. I kind of got the best of both worlds."

"Clark Kent would have been proud," Joshua said with a grin.

Amelia grinned. "Clark Kent would have been envious."

CHAPTER FOURTEEN
BAD DREAMS

The filming of the fourth and fifth movies went by uneventfully. Amelia and Joshua were getting closer to dating, and Lucas and Eva were getting closer to yelling at them to just date already. It wasn't that they hadn't come close, but even with the walls coming down, I had never seen walls come down so slowly. They played siblings, after all. Her romantic scenes with Michael put a bit of a sour note on the plans that I had for them.

Times in Hollywood were changing, though, as they always are. Amelia, Joshua, and Lucas were at the height of their popularity. Everyone knew who they were. Everyone wanted to be them. Yet there were those who despised them, despised them because everyone loved them. This is the story about how one such man decided to take fate in his hands and do something so drastic it would affect the lives of everyone involved for years to come.

The Kids' Choice Awards in Los Angeles was set for eight that night. Thoroughly used to premieres and the mania fanfare that went along with it, Amelia got ready quickly and efficiently. Award shows really were no different. She had selected a red body-con gown that night with long sleeves, finishing just under her knees. She had decided, for the first time ever, to wear, tall, black, elegant heels. Her long blond hair fluttered around her shoulders, naturally wavy from the braid it had been in all day. Still, she chose no makeup. It had become her trademark never to wear any. Many, many women admired her for it and many men liked the innocent perfection that she had. She looked stunning.

She arrived at the awards show in a limousine, as was the custom for stars, with Michael. They were due to break up next week, in Paris for the premier of the last film in the series. Finally, they would be able to see other people. Both were excited and scared by the prospect. The defense of *I have a girlfriend* was really very useful when fending off unwanted attention. They were supposed to stay friends, though. There was no awkward tension there, considering there had never been any romantic tension there. How ironic. The pair who had never been anything more than friends would go back to being what they already were. The irony of Hollywood is always palpable for me.

Michael wore a black suit, as was his custom, with a green tie. They almost looked Christmas-like in July, but the tie brought out the flecks of green in his blue eyes. He was very handsome. Amelia talked to Joshua, talked to Lucas and Eva, bounced around and talked to everyone. Over the years, she had met everyone of real importance in Hollywood, and was friends with some and tolerated others. On Michael's arm, she looked radiant and popular. She would have looked like a cheerleader in high school except for that intelligent glint in those green eyes, that glint that set her apart from everyone else there.

Jamie Hughes was there that night. He talked with his co-stars, laughed at jokes that he didn't find funny, and pretended to be among his best mates. No one in Hollywood knew about the intense hatred between the lot of them. They were actors worthy of the awards they would win. He was pleased that soon the touring and promotions would be over and he would never have to deal with them again. Not that they felt any different. There was one person he would come away missing, slightly. Amelia. She may have pranked him beyond any prank he had ever heard of. It took him weeks to get the smell out of his trailer after she was done with him, but he would miss her spunk. She certainly wasn't horrible to look at, and she was the best at pretending to be his friend when the moment arose. She didn't like him, he did not kid himself about that, but she was admirable, and under different circumstances he couldn't help but wonder if they would have been very good friends, the clever one and the devil. They would have made a nice pair. Whatever she did from here on out, he would be watching.

Amelia had been nominated for Best Actress in a Leading role, Best Actress in an Action movie, and the film itself had been nominated for two awards. She would go on to win all four awards that night, but not before something else happened. Not before someone else got in the way.

The award show was all about the kids who voted for their favorite actors, sports heroes, and films. It was important because it allowed the actors to interact with their younger fans, something our three favorite leads relished.

They walked into the giant arena and took their seats. They had all been assigned seats together, not that they were surprised. Everyone loved their chemistry. Therefore, they were typically put together. That night, though, something was off. Amelia wasn't sure what, and she wasn't sure why no one else sensed it, but something was definitely off.

The awards show began as awards shows normally do, with jokes, laughs, and bad puns. The gang was well accustomed to it all. What Amelia wasn't accustomed to was one of the steps up to the podium where she had already gone to receive two of her awards. The step looked like all the others: metal, and closed off. No one else noticed anything, but Amelia. Amelia, who had written mysteries, who had written plots sewn with deceit, Amelia knew better. The step was too rickety for its essential placement. She whispered as much to Joshua.

"Mimi, calm down. You've read too many mysteries and watched too many action movies. It's *fine.*"

Lucas said the same. "Mills, they check everyone as they come in, no one could have smuggled anything dangerous in here."

That didn't stop her from worrying. Dear reader, when a writer sniffs out a problem, listen. They can smell a plot from a mile away, and that night the plot odor was thick.

The evening went on as planned, with children screaming or laughing, with their favorite stars winning or losing. Everything was going perfectly until about an hour to the end of the show. The show was live. Suddenly every television set tuned in lost the signal. Amelia received a text from David, Joshua's brother, saying as much. She was out of her seat before Joshua could grab her arm, and that was when the ticking began: the ticking that was hooked up to every speaker in the whole arena, the ticking that suggested that Amelia, as always, had been right.

"Get everyone out!" she yelled to Joshua, before

pulling out of her heels, grabbing them in her hand and running toward the step.

"Amelia!" Lucas and Joshua yelled, seeing her running. They tried to get to her, but in vain. The crowd of screaming stars and children refused to part as they all tried to escape. Finally, fighting, Michael, Lucas, Eva, and Joshua were dragged out. Jamie had already run.

Lucas and Joshua locked eyes and in that moment they knew exactly where Amelia had gone, not that they hadn't guessed before, but seeing the same thought reflected, it made it seem all the more real. Amelia had gone to do what her character Claire would have done. Amelia had gone to hold the bomb, to cover it with herself to contain the worst of the blast. I have never seen a man more out of his mind than Joshua, shouting and attempting to rush the door, in vain. The security guards had locked it and were attempting to get everyone away from the building.

"No, no, you don't understand. Amelia, Amelia Alverson is still in there!" Joshua yelled, fighting with the guard to try to get him to unlock the digital system.

"That bomb is about to go off. You'll never get to her in time. She made her own choice," the large, bulky security guard replied, trying to get them away from the building.

This answer would not do. Lucas and Joshua locked eyes. Understanding flashed between them. They had done enough action movies together to understand what needed to be done. Joshua punched the man in the face. Lucas punched him the groin. They were in.

They dashed down the halls into the main arena where the bomb had been. They could die. They didn't care. They would die together, the golden trio to the end. They shouted her name the whole way, but received no response. The ticking was still going. They found the big room, and ran in. She was curled around the box that she must have extracted from the step. Her hands moved— in prayer, they thought. They soon realized that she was playing with the bomb. The ticking stopped. They were right next to her. She looked up.

"Amelia Katherine Alverson, what have you gotten us into this time?" Lucas demanded. Her face, tense from a moment before, relaxed.

"The ticking, it's stopped," Joshua said, looking around.

"That would be because I deactivated the bomb," Amelia said, looking quite pleased with herself as Joshua pulled her to her feet. "And who told you my middle name?"

"Of bloody *course* you did," Lucas heaved, pulling the two of them into a hug.

"There was a switch. No good bomb maker doesn't install a switch."

She breathed out. Her relief was clear. Watching the military channel for years with her father had finally paid off. The guys should have been surprised—it wasn't a well-known skill—but they had known her too long to ever be surprised anymore.

That was when the bomb squadron chose to run in. The sight they found, the three best friends, hugging, exchanging stories, laughing over the fact that she had done it, that Amelia had saved them all, was not what they had expected.

"You know, I never really noticed how very like Claire you are," Lucas said.

"I still can't believe you guys just punched the security guard," she said. A smile decorated her face. Her eyes were the ornaments.

"He wouldn't let us in!" Joshua exclaimed.

"He was just doing his job!" she said. She could have been cross with them. Most people would have been, but honestly, she was too happy to be alive with them by her side to care.

Joshua got quiet though for a moment and looked at her.

"Ams, are you okay?"

"I'm alive," she replied.

His eyes searched hers. "That wasn't what I asked." She looked away.

If there was a silver lining, it was that the cameras had gone live again, appearing on millions of television sets in the world again, right before Amelia deactivated the bomb. The world had seen everything, but more importantly they had seen their three favorite action heroes be the action heroes they were always meant to be. Everything was just as it should have been.

"I can't believe you did that."

"Josh, I wasn't just going to run outside and let it happen, let hundreds of people die when I could have prevented it," Amelia said, aghast. The awards show had been hours ago and Joshua had come to see her in her hotel room.

"Why did you have to do it, though? That's what security guards are for!" Joshua exclaimed.

"And my life is somehow worth more than theirs?" Amelia demanded, shocked.

"To me, yes."

Amelia laughed, scornfully. "I don't think it matters what you think or who you value more. It's my life and my choice to make. I'm not your girlfriend, you're not my parents, and frankly I don't think anyone should have the right to tell me what I can and can't do!"

"Amelia, you're a celebrity—" Joshua started to say.

"Exactly. I must be counted upon to make the right choices, to do what I think is best. I've never wanted any of this fame, but if it makes people realize that putting others first is the right thing to do, then maybe it was all worth it. Being a celebrity shouldn't be about wearing fancy clothing and dating the hottest actors. If children are going to look up to you, then you should give them something to look up to. Clearly, we disagree on that front."

"You can't just put yourself in danger like that! I won't let you!" Joshua exclaimed.

"I don't recall asking your permission!" Amelia yelled. "Plus, you went running back in there, too and you don't see me trying to stop you!"

"I went running back because you were there. What did you expect me to do? Leave you alone? Watch you die? I didn't know you could stop the explosion. How was I supposed to know that?" Joshua asked.

"You were supposed to trust me! In every interview, in everything that we do, we *always* talk about how much we trust each other, how we're all best friends. I knew everything in Hollywood was fake, I just didn't realize *that* was," Amelia said, shaking her head.

"None of that is fake! How is that fair, to ask me that? To pretend like our friendship is nothing to me when we aren't in front of a camera?" Joshua demanded.

"You grew up in Hollywood. I didn't, and yet even I know that *nothing* here is fair."

Amelia awoke to shrieking. The actors were in their hotel rooms in Amsterdam, sleeping. The premier would be the next night. The crisis with the Kids' Choice Awards had been a month ago. The actors were to continue with their plan as if nothing had happened, only something *had* happened. There was no denying it. Anyway, as I was saying, Amelia woke up to screaming in the hotel room to her right. That was Joshua's hotel room. And that was Joshua's voice, she was sure of it. She was out of bed so fast you would have thought a fire alarm sounded. She didn't bother to grab a robe or anything as she sprinted out of her room into the hallway where she saw a maid walking by.

The screaming had stopped. The maid acted as if she hadn't heard anything. Amelia's heart began to beat very fast.

"Excuse me, would you mind opening the door? I have a tendency to sleepwalk and I must have come out here."

The maid nodded, unlocking the door to Josh's room and Amelia dashed in, shutting it in the maid's face and not even caring about being rude. She ran straight over to the bed where Joshua was writhing under the sheets that entrapped him. It had been a month since their argument, a month since they had spoken.

"Josh, Josh, what's wrong?" she asked, shaking him awake.

His eyes flew open at her gentle shaking. "Ams!" he gasped.

"Josh, what happened? You were screaming your

head off and the maid outside wasn't doing anything and I had to lie and tell her that this was my room, and good gosh, Josh! Was someone stabbing you?" she said, all in one breath, her heartbeat calming down at seeing him wholly unharmed.

"I was screaming out loud, Ams?" he asked, sitting up and clapping his hands so that the lights in the room would turn on.

"Like someone was trying to kill you," she said, the concern still palpable in her voice.

"Ams, you heard me screaming. You thought I was getting stabbed and you ran in here empty-handed?" he asked, surveying her empty hands that were on his shoulders, sending electric currents through him.

"Okay, I admit I didn't really think it through, but I heard you yelling and I just ran, hoping that I could come up with a solution when I needed to," she said, sheepishly. "Why were you screaming, anyway?"

He looked at her. She wore short Under Armour shorts and a Giants baseball t-shirt. Her blond hair fell around her shoulders and her feet were bare. She was in his bed, in his room. Anything could happen, and boy, did he want it to. He felt such a deep passion for her. Every fiber in his being told him to kiss her, but his brain reminded him that she had a boyfriend, even if she didn't like him. For media purposes, she had a boyfriend. That meant she was off-limits.

Perhaps he could have taken her. Perhaps she might not have stopped him, but even after this long, he knew that he wanted her to want it as much as he did. She was right here, though, with her hands on him. He made a conscious effort to meet her eyes. Little did he know that she too was looking him over. Joshua slept in boxers, nothing else. His chest was bare, revealing the TN tattoo on his side. His hair was messy but that gorgeous kind of messy that made her want to fix it.

"Bad dream," he said finally.

"What about?" she asked, trying not to feel too attracted by those gorgeous brown eyes.

"The bombing. Even though it was a month ago, I just can't get it out of my head," he said. She moved around on the bed so that she was sitting next to him. The desire was there. You could feel the sexual tension, it was so palpable. There were just too many restraints.

"The bomber is locked up in prison, Josh. He'll never get out," she said, looking up at him. She wanted to fix that hair so bad, so incredibly bad, but she used every ounce of strength she had and resisted. Boys break your heart. She didn't want her heart broken again. It had been so hard to put back together the first time.

"I know that, but Ams, Ams, you almost *died*. How can you be okay after a thing like that?" he asked. She had a strand of blond hair on her cheek and he wanted nothing more than to move it and lean in to kiss her. But he couldn't.

"I know that. I didn't die, though, so it's okay," she said. Truthfully? She had been freaking out on the inside ever since then. The right people didn't know how she felt about them and that was scary. As always, though, she couldn't let on. She had to be brave to the bitter end.

"We all would have died, but you saved us. You were willing to give your life for all of us to live. You dove on that bomb and turned it off. You had no idea if you could turn it off or not, but you still dove on it," Joshua said quietly.

"And that bothers you?" she asked.

"Yes, because I should have been the one diving on the bomb. I never should have let you be put in any kind of danger," he said. His voice was clear, unlike his mind.

He was too sweet, too perfect, and exactly what she wanted, except she couldn't let herself have him. He deserved better, she felt, and plus, there was no way *he* liked *her*. Guys never liked her. They never had. Why would the most perfect guy she had ever met be any different?

"Get some sleep, Josh. We have another premier tomorrow. I promise if there's a bomb, I'll let you have it," she said. It was no joking matter, but she didn't want to tell him why she had dived on the bomb: because a world without him wasn't a world she wanted to be in. If she said that, then it would be flirting and she couldn't flirt, not with him. If she let herself fall for him, then she knew herself well enough to know that there would be no coming back. Him not loving her back would kill her.

He didn't want her to leave, by any means. He was a twenty-eight-year old man unable to settle down because the one girl he had loved for the past four years of his life didn't love him back, at least to his knowledge.

"Okay."

"Do you want me to stay? Until you fall asleep, that is," she asked. She didn't want to leave. She loved being around him.

Yes.

"No, I'm okay. Thank you for waking me up, otherwise I would still be in that horrible dream. And, Ams... I'm sorry about what I said, about how you never should have dived on the bomb. You were right. The choice was yours to make, not mine. I do trust you. I've always trusted you."

"I appreciate you caring, Josh. Just know that I will always make my own choices, dangerous as they might be. Don't let it bother you. If I ever get myself killed, remember that I did it on my own terms. And, it was no problem, waking you up. Goodnight." With that, she walked out the door, leaving him wishing he could fall asleep with her in his arms, leaving her wishing he had asked her to stay.

Amelia had just tucked herself back into bed in her

hotel room when there was a knock on the door. She had left Joshua's room five minutes ago and come back here, paced for five minutes, chastising herself over the way she had acted. She had always vowed that she wouldn't be like the girls in the movies who got mad at the guys when there wasn't a need. Of course she could protect herself, and him telling her that she couldn't was ridiculous, but he was coming from the right place.

She switched on her lamp and didn't even bother throwing on a bathrobe before she threw open the door, expecting to see one of the maids asking her some silly question.

"Josh?"

"Ams, can I come in?"

She paused only a second before opening the door and stepping aside to let him in. "Is everything okay, Josh?"

"Why do you always have to pretend like you aren't scared?" he demanded as she shut the door and turned to look at him. He was still in his boxer shorts.

"What?" she asked, taken aback.

"Ever since I've met you, you always seem to be the perfect blend of calm and happy and not afraid, never afraid. We live in a bubble, a bubble where everyone is scrutinizing our every mistake, our every decision, and evaluating it on thousands upon thousands of websites. We have to have security guards with us everywhere because people mob us, and who's not to say that one day, one day the guards won't be enough and the mob will hurt us? Who's not to say that you didn't know how to detonate that bomb? Who's not to say that you ran in there for some other reason? Who's not to say that you weren't scared out of your mind to do it?" he asked. His brown eyes met her green ones.

She laughed a humorless laugh. "Isn't this when you're supposed to tell me that it's okay to be scared, that being scared is a part of life?"

He shook his head, calming down instantly. "No, this is where I tell you that you don't need to pretend to be brave, not for me."

"Easier said than done."

"No. Ams, you're my best friend. It shouldn't have to be easier said than done," Joshua said, with a slight smile.

"I'm not very good at being honest about my emotions," she replied.

"Well, Little Miss Perfect, I think you should work on that."

She laughed. "Maybe I should."

"Do you want to start now?"

"I don't think I've ever been honest about my emotions in my whole life. I guess I've always assumed that I have to be brave, that I have to be above fear and sadness, and above pain. That I have to pretend like pain and all those thoughts that come with it don't exist."

"How's that been working out for you?"

"Really badly, actually."

"Well then there you go! Don't work so hard to pretend that pain doesn't reach you. Don't be so above me that I can't reach you."

"Josh, why didn't you tell anyone that I was scared, scared to dive on the bomb? You were right; I didn't know how to detonate it. I just knew that if I didn't do something that I would never leave that room, not really. I'd be trapped in the past forever trying to find a way to save the people that would have died, to overcome my cowardliness," Amelia said, softly.

Joshua shrugged. "Because I don't think being scared is something bad. I think it makes you human, and I want you to be human."

"Why?"

"Because then, then you don't seem like you're a million light years ahead of me, because then I don't feel like I'm never going to be good enough," he said. "Because, maybe, if you're human, if you get scared, if you feel pain, then maybe you aren't so far away from me."

Amelia did something that he wasn't expecting then: she threw her arms around him and gave him a hug. "I was never far away from you. You were just always looking ahead and never to the side."

Joshua went back to his room five minutes later,

comforted in their friendship, but hurt by the romantic
separation that still bound them from each other.

CHAPTER FIFTEEN
ENGLAND

The series was over. All of the movies had been made, all of the premieres had been attended, all of the tickets had sold, and all of the actors had said goodbye, parting as friends, or in Jamie and Joshua's case: acquaintances. It was all over.

Amelia had always told Joshua that once the films were over, she would move to England. He just hadn't believed her.

"Is L.A. not good enough for you? Is that it?"

"Josh, don't be ridiculous. You know that I've always wanted to live in England. You *know* that. It's not as if I'm springing this on you. I told you ages ago that this is how it would be," Amelia said, throwing her hands up in frustration.

She had come back to her apartment to say goodbye and had found Joshua there. He had been sitting in the middle of the empty room that had been the living room, reading her latest novel. Her pulse had spiked at seeing that, but her anger had spiked at what he would say. They had been arguing for twenty minutes now. She needed to leave or she would miss her flight.

"What do they have there that I can't offer you here? What is so special about England that I have to lose my two best friends to it?" he asked. He didn't understand why she wouldn't stay.

"A job? Josh, I've been offered my *dream* job. I get to be on my favorite show from when I was a teenager. They offered me a pivotal role and I owe it to myself then to take it now. What's so hard to understand about that?" she demanded.

"Your family is in America."

"My family is coming *there*. My parents, they're getting a flat in London. They're going to spend half their time there, half their time in San Francisco. They've already got the flat, and they rarely ever come to Los Angeles. I'll get to see them more than I have in years. My sister is planning on moving there once she graduates college, so there won't be anyone left here for me."

"I'll be here."

"You'll be busy doing movies and being you. Lucas and Eva will be in England. I have a job in England. I have to be in England," she replied, quietly.

"No, you don't. No job is worth leaving everything."

"Josh, you are one of my best friends and you know that this is what I have always wanted, but you don't want me to go?" Amelia demanded.

"I'm in love with you."

"I don't think you are."

"Oh yeah? What would you know about love? I don't even think you have a heart!" Joshua shouted. It was childish, but he was mad.

"I know enough to know that when you love someone you support them, and what you're doing right now? It's not support. Goodbye, Joshua. It was nice knowing you."

And with that, Amelia walked out the door to go catch her flight to England, thinking that she would never see Joshua again. She wasn't okay with it, not on an emotional level, but on a pragmatic level she realized that if she wasn't going to commit to him, this might be her only chance to set him free.

She wouldn't have seen him, either, except for Lucas. Remember how I told you he would be important? This is his bit.

Joshua was so angry that he picked up Amelia's most recent novel and threw it against the wall of her empty apartment in disgust. When he did, a paper fell onto the floor. He didn't want to check who the note was from—he was too mad—so instead he sat in the middle of the empty room and sulked for an hour, hoping it or his anger would go away. Her flight was just now taking off. He was angry but still curious and so he went over and picked it up. It was an envelope with a note from Lucas inside.

Hullo Joshua,

If you are reading this then you and Amy have had the fight Eva and I suspected you would have. Anyway, you stupidly told her you loved her and she didn't say it back which made you mad and you said some nasty things. The thing is, mate, when you tell someone you love them, it can't be the words you think will hold them back. You do love her. Eva and I believe that. You just need a little help. She's moving to England for her dream job surrounded by attractive men with accents. You're going to continue living in Los Angeles, a city full of beautiful girls unless the only girl you love isn't there. Since you love her with the kind of love that stirs the seas, you only have two options:

1. Let her go.
2. Follow her.

I have a plane ticket to London for you enclosed here to help you make the right decision. If I know you and your incredible sense of timing, your flight leaves in an hour.

She loves you. I believe that in my heart. So don't tell her you love her. Show her. If you don't believe me, check the first page of this book. The choice is yours. I just hope you make the right one.

The address is enclosed. Knowing Amy, we will be unpacking late.

London is beautiful this time of year. I hope you come see it,

> *Luc*

Joshua opened the last novel in the *Aliens* series. He had read it many times but had always flipped to where the story began. He found himself faced with the dedication.

To Josh: Thank you for being my best friend. And to Luc, for always knowing the right thing to say.

And dear reader, once again, Lucas had known the right thing to say.

There wouldn't be a real love story if he didn't get on that plane, so I guess it's a good thing there wasn't much traffic that night. You might even say someone helped clear the streets. You might even say the streets were clear because everyone knew why he needed them to be on that warm night. So, with nothing packed, Joshua drove like he wanted a ticket to that airport. Lucky for him, Lucas had planned for this and brought some things with him.

The plane was delayed. It was raining, hard. Joshua hated rain. He hated everything wet. Why did it need to rain? Why did this infernal rain need to stop him from going after her? Sure, the plane could crash because of the storm, but the plane might also *not* crash and he might get to England sooner. He was willing to take the risk. Clearly, no one else was.

"Hey mate, could you stop pacing, for like two seconds, please?" a young man with jet-black hair said, looking up at Joshua. If he recognized him, he didn't let on. So far, Joshua had been left alone to pace, until now.

Joshua stopped and looked at him. "I like to pace."

"And I like some bloke in large jumper to not keep entering my peripheral vision every minute and a half making me think I'm going to be arrested by Scotland Yard," the man replied.

"Excuse me, did you just imply that you are a convict and that the police are coming for you?" Joshua asked, confused.

"What are you going to England for?" the man said, ignoring Joshua's question.

"See a friend."

"What kind of friend?"

"A very good one."

"Well then, would you mind not looking so bloody nervous? Your friend will still be there if we land three hours later, I guarantee it."

"Well, I don't," Joshua replied, his voice bitter.

"So you're going to London," the woman next to Joshua commented. Gray hair reached only to her neck in curls. She had gray eyes and wrinkled skin—no attempt at makeup, though, no attempt to hide her age. That was new for someone coming out of Los Angeles. She was elderly, probably in her early eighties and yet there was something about her that reminded him of youth.

"Yes, I am. As are you," he said, trying to look out the window and demonstrate his disdain for the conversation to be prolonged. He could hardly wait to see Amelia. Lucas had gotten him the worst seats in the whole plane, all the way in the back, right next to the bathroom. There was even a crying baby a row over, though how Lucas had known that escaped Joshua.

The woman refused to be rebuked. "Who's the girl?"

Joshua was used to being recognized, he was used to being talked to as if he had known someone their whole life. He was used to being followed and hit on, and any number of other creepy things that came with being famous. But never, never in his whole life had he seen the look of amusement at his expense, so complete, as he was being given by this elderly woman.

"Excuse me?" he asked, giving up on looking out the window completely. He searched her eyes. She didn't know who he was. Maybe she lived under a rock. But she seemed to know his situation.

"There's a girl," she replied, still smiling like she knew something he didn't. Had Lucas called ahead and told her something?

"There's no girl." Joshua was a professional liar— he did this for a living. He just needed to act like he was playing a character, a character who didn't know Amelia and wasn't in love with her.

"There's always a girl," the old woman replied, shaking her head slowly in amusement.

"Well, not this time," he said, shaking his head, smiling at her in what he hoped was also an amused way so that she would believe him.

She smiled and put her hand on his thigh. "Son, it's a thirteen-hour flight. You might as well tell me about her."

So, resigning himself to his fate, he did.

"She sounds lovely," the woman said, smiling when he was done.

"Thank you," he replied. He felt better now. He always did after talking about Amelia.

"Son, never tell a girl that whatever it is she wants

to do, it doesn't matter. She will leave you for whatever it is," the old woman said.

"I learned that the hard way," he acknowledged. "I just didn't understand why she had to leave me by myself."

"People want to be needed. You didn't show her you needed her, so she left. It hurts not to be needed," the woman replied. "Always tell her you love her and you need her, and go get her."

"Thank you, I will. So what brings you to London?"

"A whim."

Moments later, Joshua fell asleep. When he awoke, the old woman was gone. He asked the stewardess, but she said no one had been sitting there the entire flight. She had been a blessing, or someone else in disguise. She might even have been me, but we'll get to that later.

Amelia had left Joshua behind. It was for the better. She had let him go. It hurt, though. It felt like there was a hole in her stomach where her heart should have been, like all the oxygen from her lungs had left her and now her lungs and her heart were empty. She wanted Joshua there more than anything she had ever wanted in her life, but she had let him go and now he was gone. It was for the better—only for whose better she wasn't sure she knew anymore.

The entire flight, she had run their conversation over and over again in her mind: how he had said he loved her, how she had left him there, mad. She had never wanted to end things with anyone mad, and yet she had, with one of her best friends in the whole world. She had left mad.

Would she ever see him again? Probably in newspapers or magazines, but that wouldn't be enough. Would she ever hear his voice again? Would she ever see him smile as he looked at her? She doubted it, she really did, and there was nothing more painful than doubt.

Should she have done it differently? Should she have told him that she loved him back? She had never told anyone that she loved them. It would have been hard to get the words out, and yet she was sure that she could have, for him. Should she have stayed? Should she have given up her golden rule: lives before guys? If she were going to give it up for anyone, it would have been him. She had made a mistake, a very big mistake, and there was no way that she could fix it.

"Amy, there's someone outside for you," Lucas said, glancing out the window that looked out on the street and Tower Bridge. He continued putting books, her Dickens collection, from a box on one of the shelves of her flat.

"Who?" she asked, wiping her brow. She wore ripped blue jeans and a navy tank top. Her hair was pulled back into a silky ponytail.

"Just go." Lucas rolled his eyes and tried to hide his smile.

"Thanks for the mystery, Holmes," she said, rolling her eyes in turn. She walked out onto the little porch out front of her house. There was no one there.

"Luc, there's no one here!" she shouted, before seeing a figure standing a few feet away on the entrance of the bridge. "Josh?"

"Sorry I'm late. Are there any boxes left to unpack?" he asked.

"You—" she started to say before forgetting about it and running to him. He caught her in his arms and spun her.

"I missed you, Ams," he said, hugging her close to him. "I understand that you don't want to date, and it hurts bad to be around you, but it hurts worse to not be around you at all. So, if you're prepared to forgive me, I want to be your friend again."

"You idiot, you've been my best friend from the moment we met," she said as he put her down. She looked into his eyes that were illuminated by the street lamps on the bridge.

"So it won't be weird for you that I'm in love with you?" he asked.

She looked at him and did something so unexpected that he almost lost his balance and fell into the river below. She kissed him, full on the mouth, a kiss to top all kisses, one full of passion and adoration.

"Only if you're okay with me being in love with you,

too," she said, smiling into his mouth. It was the first time he had ever heard her say it.

"It's not weird," he said.

"But you live in L.A. and I live here," she said, this detail coming back to her. "Long distance almost never works out."

"They have other houses in England. As you said: you live here," he said.

"You could live with me," she suggested.

"If you'll have me," he said.

"I have plenty of room. Come on, knowing you, you brought no furniture. Let me show you our new house," she said, lacing her hand through his and walking him back to what was now their house.

"What a way to go, we go from not dating and living on separate continents to dating and living in the same house," Joshua said with a laugh.

"Keep up, Clemons. This, this is Hollywood. Everything, everything happens in between the flashes of a camera," Amelia said, smiling up at him.

Lucas stood on the front stoop. With Eva in his arms, he looked toward them and smiled. "Only took the guy seven years to get the girl."

"He could have done worse," Eva said, attempting to hide her smile.

"He could have done it *faster*," Lucas said, also fighting back a grin.

CHAPTER SIXTEEN
BAKER STREET

"Those two will literally drive me mad," Lucas said, throwing his phone down on the couch next to Eva before flopping on after it.

She laughed and ruffled his hair. "I think it's cute."

"Cute? Cute? You disgust me. There is nothing cute about deciding to go to Manchester for the weekend without telling their best friend," Lucas replied, indignant.

"Amelia never has time off. They should use this little bit of time to get away," Eva said.

"Actually, they should spend it with me, or at least bother to tell me of their plans!" he exclaimed.

"Honey, they left you a voicemail," Eva replied, rolling her eyes.

"They left me a voicemail. Well, that's brilliant,

except NO ONE LEAVES VOICEMAILS. People *text*. Why? Why do people text, you ask?" he asked, sitting up so that he could look at her.

"I didn't ask," she replied, doing her best to hide her smile.

"Well, I will tell you. People text so that no one has to check a voicemail where the person is probably mumbling bad news into the phone because no one delivers good news through a voicemail, and instead, they can allow the person to *read* the bad news in a sentence or less," Lucas replied, dramatically.

"I don't think they thought it was bad news," Eva pointed out, still trying to hide her smile.

"I brought a six pack of beer and a movie to watch and there was no one there. I had to come home and watch the movie alone. That is very bad news," Lucas replied slowly.

"How horrible," Eva replied in mock sympathy.

"Well, you know what? Next time you want to watch *The Notebook*, you can do it without *me*," Lucas replied, getting up and stomping out.

"I'll leave you a voicemail with what happens," she replied with a laugh.

"*Text!*" Lucas yelled from the other room.

"Luky-Luc, Manchester wasn't a last-minute plan. We had talked about it for a month," Amelia said, rolling her eyes.

"Maybe *you* two did," he replied.

"No, we told you, too. Do you ever listen when I talk?" she asked, laughing.

"Absolutely not," Lucas replied, pulling her to him and kissing her on the head.

"You're such a deaf idiot," she replied, still laughing, but she didn't pull away.

"Now, Joshua, what is this I hear about you buying a house on Baker Street?" Lucas pressed.

Lucas, Eva, Amelia, and Joshua were walking back to Amelia's flat off Tower Bridge. They had just come from dinner at their favorite restaurant right in front of the Tower of London, a stir-fry place. It was November in London, six months after they had moved there. Lucas wore blue jeans and a long brown trench coat with boots. Eva wore tall, black, heeled boots, a scarf, a beanie, and a large, but not too large, purple coat with black jeans. Joshua wore a large black coat, blue jeans, and boots. Amelia wore a scarf, a beanie, combat boots, skinny dark blue jeans, and a large blue coat. They all wore gloves. It wasn't snowing out, but that didn't mean that it wasn't cold.

"Who told you about that?" Joshua asked, laughing as he pulled Amelia away from Lucas and back to him, spinning her and causing her to laugh all the more. He watched her and I saw myself reflected in his eyes.

"Please, my country, my city, I'm all-knowing," Lucas replied, rolling his eyes.

"Right," Eva scoffed. He shoved her lightly and she laughed.

"No, but really though, is everything okay with you two?" he asked. His voice grew serious.

"Aren't you supposed to ask that with me not here?" Amelia asked, amused.

"Probably, but then I would have to pick who to ask, and, well, this just seemed so much easier," Lucas replied.

"Everything is amazing, actually." Joshua replied.

"His parents are just coming to visit more and more now, and our little flat just doesn't have the room," Amelia explained.

"She actually picked out the house," Joshua added, smiling fondly at his girlfriend.

"She did?" Eva asked, looking over at Amelia and smiling. That was a big deal in any relationship: picking out a house.

"Yeah, she wanted Baker Street because of Sherlock Holmes. It's a big—well, city-big—white house with columns. It's in between two other houses. Basically the whole street—all the houses—-are connected on the outside. The inside is really nice though, five bedrooms, four baths. It's great. We can always stay there, too, whenever we feel like the flat is too small, or when we want to host parties," Joshua replied, smiling.

"I'm assuming I will be invited to these parties?" Lucas asked.

"If you're lucky," Amelia replied.

It had happened. Joshua had gotten to the point in his life where Amelia was indispensable. She would have to go for filming in Cardiff for long periods of time, working on her latest novels in between takes, but he didn't mind. He would go with her and stay there, making other friends around the city to see, but never missing their breakfasts and dinners together. Even when things got crazy, they never missed those.

At breakfast, they would tell each what they were going to do that day and at dinner, they would tell each other what had actually happened. Joshua found other acting jobs in England. Soon he was signed up to be in a play in the West End. It was a big deal. He had never done stage acting in his life, but he was excited to try. This meant he would be in London all day for work. No matter. He took the train back to Cardiff, never missing their two meals together. They would both help with breakfast, switching around who made what. Dinner, though, dinner Amelia made.

Joshua claimed it was because he wasn't a very good cook. This wasn't true, though. If she was exhausted, then he had no problem making dinner. Most of the time he liked it when she made dinner because he loved watching

195

her cook from the breakfast bar in their kitchen. He loved the little creases that would appear in her brow as she concentrated, and the look of complete and utter pleasure when he took a bite and told her it was delicious. He never missed a chance to tell her it was delicious, never. That smile made his day. He also never missed a chance to do the dishes.

He loved doing the dishes, strangely enough. It wasn't hard. She cleaned her plate when she put it in the sink, but he always dragged it out because she would sit on the counter in front of him and tell stories, true stories, or stories she invented. It didn't matter, not really. They were always good. I would stop by whenever I could spare a moment to listen to her stories, too.

"Jonathan raced down the street, not caring who was behind him, only caring about what was in front of him. If the cops caught him then they would have enough to put him in prison: the stolen bread was in his very hands. He could throw it away, in theory at least, but he was so hungry, so desperately hungry that he couldn't actually throw it away, not without throwing part of himself with it. He leapt over the trashcan, down the alley where he realized just how futile the whole thing had been. The cops were right behind him, closer than he had anticipated, and he was trapped, woefully trapped. Josh, are you done?"

This isn't all to say that they were the perfect couple,

or that they agreed on everything and were always happy. They didn't always agree, by a long shot. But most of their arguments stemmed from something that was upsetting to them about the other one.

"How come you won't call me 'babe'? Eva calls Lucas 'babe' all the time. Most couples call each other that, so why don't we?"

"Josh, you *know* why. It makes me super uncomfortable, like the whole 'who's your daddy' thing. It's weird and I don't like it. I'm fine with nicknames. I like nicknames, just so long as those don't get weird, but as far as calling you 'babe,' don't expect that any time soon."

"It's just I feel like other couples judge us for it."

"So what if they do? I don't care. Just because I don't call you a synonym for an infant child doesn't mean our entire relationship is invalidated."

Overall though, there was never anything big that they argued about. They had been such good friends for so long that they had both known what they were getting into. They knew each other's limits and they did their best not to push them. Besides the whole "babe" thing, they were a fairly ordinary couple, except for one small, teensy detail.

"You two haven't had sex yet?"

"Luc, she doesn't want to. She's religious; she wants to save herself for marriage and all that."

"That's horridly inconvenient."

"Look, I don't like it, but I respect it. It's her choice and I have no right to make it for her."

"Wait, so what is the sleeping arrangement for you two?"

"Separate rooms."

"You're kidding. Couldn't you sleep next to her, at least?"

"Dude, this was my choice."

"Oh, did you do it to get back at her?"

"Heck no. I did this because I can't sleep next to her and not want to take it further. I did it as a precaution. I'd go medically insane just sleeping next to her and not being able to kiss her or anything for fear it would escalate."

"Wow, you must really love her, mate."

"I do."

He did. He had considered many times threatening to leave if she wouldn't give this to him because he wasn't sure they were compatible in that way, in a way that mattered. And yet whenever he had considered saying the words out loud to her he would glance over and she would be giving him her full attention, hanging on to his every word, and he just couldn't. He couldn't risk leaving her and wondering about what could have been, not when he loved her this much, not when he had waited this long. And so, he stayed.

Being a celebrity couple was far from easy. Your whole relationship is in a fishbowl under scrutiny from the whole world constantly. It broke up a lot of couples. Being one of the most popular and famous celebrity couples? That was near impossible. Joshua and Amelia had their work cut out for them.

"Apparently you're pregnant now?"

"Third time this week. I really wish someone would tell me before they would tell the tabloids."

"Pregnant and not even married. Tsk, tsk."

"How very scandalous. Is the child at least yours this time?"

"Nope, too mainstream. It's Luc's."

"Oh my gosh, can I please frame that? That is so priceless it needs to be in a frame."

"No one told *Palace* it was priceless. Considering that it is priceless, I'm really glad I snatched it up for five pounds."

"You got lucky."

"Should I go buy fifty more? Sell my house? Buy all of them?"

"You could retire off the profits you'll make from selling them."

"That's exactly what I was thinking."

They were so used to it, so calm by what would drive most people mad. They almost found it funny to pretend to be James Bond and hide from the paparazzi, laughing themselves silly.

"Quick, the paps!"

"Behind the bush!"

"Did you just jump over a bush? That's the greatest escape plan I've ever seen!" Amelia exclaimed as she looked around the street and grinned at the waiter of the restaurant whose bush Joshua had just jumped behind. The guy shrugged like it happened every day and walked off with his drink tray.

"Um, I make jumping behind bushes look fabulous." He posed. "Don't you wish your boyfriend was hot like me?"

"All the time. Seriously, thank you for reminding me about the bush. They're everywhere. I'll have to remember that trick."

"You're welcome. Leaves are tricky for cameras. It's a handy trick I've learned over the years."

"Of course it is."

"There were no paparazzi, were there?"

"You are so much fun to mess with."

"Yeah, yeah, yeah, no but seriously, I think that guy with the camera phone over there got all that on film."

"Josh, that guy with the camera phone is Luc with a hat."

"Am I on a celebrity pranking show?"

"Yeah, it's called the Amelia-and-Lucas-make-

Joshua-look-like-an-idiot show. My new favorite program."

"Nice to see you too, Luc."

The paparazzi were never sure what to do with them. They followed them. Sometimes they got photos, and sometimes they came up with nothing. Amelia and Joshua had a reputation for running into museums and pretending to be the historical mannequins as the men raced past with their cameras. They really couldn't have cared less about getting their photo taken; they just thought it was fun to make it a game, so make it a game they did. The amount of fame they had should have driven them mad. Instead, they found themselves having more fun than ever before. Sometimes it was a bit much, the attention, but it was the cost of acting—the opportunity cost of doing something that they were passionate about. An opportunity cost that they didn't have a choice in paying.

CHAPTER SEVENTEEN
TOWER BRIDGE

"Will you marry me?"

Joshua was down on one knee in front of Lucas in Lucas and Eva's living room, a ring in a box in hand.

"Oh of *course*. Darling, I thought you'd *never* ask!" Lucas exclaimed with a high-pitched southern drawl.

Joshua stood up, closing the box. "Is that how you think Amelia talks?"

"Um, that's how I *know* Amelia talks, mate," Lucas replied, resuming his regular voice.

"She doesn't even have a southern accent," Joshua pointed out.

"Yeah but how much better would it be if she did?" Lucas asked, walking into the kitchen to grab an apple. He grabbed a second one and threw it to Joshua who was prepared for this and caught it, taking a bite out of it.

"Juicy," he commented.

Lucas nodded as if the compliment had been directed towards him. "I can't believe you're *finally* going to ask her."

"It's been a year. That's super short for dating to marriage time," Joshua pointed out. This was a point of concern for him. He knew it was right but would Amelia want to wait? To date longer? Her parents had dated for three years before her father had popped the question. Would she want to wait the same amount of time?

"Yeah, I know that, but I mean, it's *you* and *her*. You've been in love with her from the moment you two met. I swear you would have proposed before she even opened her mouth to talk to you and yet you waited all this time," Lucas replied, rolling his eyes and taking a bite of his apple.

"I would not have proposed before she opened her mouth," Joshua replied, skeptically. It was false skeptical. He knew as well as Lucas that he would have. The only thing that stopped him was the fact that he didn't have a ring.

"Mate," Lucas said, giving him a look.

"Shut up," Joshua replied, basically admitting defeat.

"My favorite part was her asking you about your tramp stamp," Lucas said, sitting on his couch, continuing to work on his apple.

Lucas hadn't actually been there when the tramp stamp was asked about. He had been elsewhere at the party. But the story had been repeated often in the media, especially when Amelia and Joshua began dating. It was probably Lucas's all-time favorite story. He had asked them to tell it so many times that now they refused to. He loved it all the more and now he would tell it to virtually anyone who would listen.

"You will never be over that, will you?" Joshua asked, sounding resigned as he sat down on the couch alongside his buddy. In reality, he was amused. He loved hearing about the first time he met Amelia, too, even if he had been there.

Whenever he heard it, he couldn't help but remember how nervous and excited he had felt around her. The nervousness had calmed over the years but the excitement had only grown. She was as beautiful to him as the day they met, and a whole lot more interesting.

"She put you in your place then and she's been putting you in your place ever since," Lucas said, smiling broadly.

"That she has," Joshua said, smiling at the thought of how feisty Amelia was, before adding as an afterthought, though it wasn't an afterthought, "Do you think she'll accept?"

Lucas was quiet for a moment, a long moment, so

long Joshua thought it would never end and that he would have to listen to his own hammering heart forever when finally Lucas replied, "She loves you."

"That doesn't answer my question," Joshua said.

"Actually, it does," Lucas replied.

It did, too. It answered the real question behind what Joshua had asked: "Does she love me?" It answered it to perfection, actually. That was what best mates are for, though: answering the questions you don't ask as well as the questions that you do.

Joshua was quiet for a long while. "I think I'm going to propose on Tower Bridge."

"Smart lad," Lucas commented.

Tower Bridge was often confused for London Bridge, something Amelia, who had built Tower Bridge out of Legos, found maddening. She loved building and architecture and she loved, loved, loved Tower Bridge. That was the reason she had bought a flat where she could see it at all times. It was also the place where she had first told Joshua she loved him. Really, it seemed like the logical spot.

"Thanks."

"When are you going to do it?" Lucas asked. He had finished his apple now and was making drawings on what was left of it with his thumb.

"Tonight. We have a romantic dinner at our favorite restaurant and then we're going for a walk," Joshua replied, sounding out of breath.

"Nervous?" Lucas asked.

"Not in the least bit," Joshua replied.

"You know, I know why she trusts you so much now," Lucas said.

"Why?" Joshua asked, confused at the change in topic.

"Because you're the worst liar ever and she will always know when you're up to something."

"That's going to pose a bit of a problem for my acting career."

"Trust me, it already does."

"Joshua, are you up to something?"

"I'm never up to anything. What are you talking about?" he asked, grinning as he took her hand.

She looked beautiful with her blond hair cascading around her face, and her bright green eyes brought out by her green long-sleeve shirt. She wore black skinny jeans and blue ballerina flats to match, with a navy scarf around her neck. It wasn't there because it was cold, though. It was late May in London, six months after they had all arrived, and the air was growing warmer outside. The sun was actually shining that day. She wore what she wore because, despite everything else, she was always cold. It was one of Joshua's favorite things about her. Because she was always cold, she always needed someone to make her warm and he knew just the person. Joshua, on the other hand, who didn't mind the cold, or at this point, a slight breeze, wore a white V-necked shirt, dark blue jeans, and black combat boots. He looked handsome to Amelia, and to every other girl walking the streets of London that night. It wasn't quite dark yet. The sun would be setting in a few minutes, and in a few minutes Joshua planned to be on the bridge to watch it happen.

"Actually, you're always up to something," Amelia corrected. She let him take her hand, though, smiling at him out of the corner of her eye as she pretended to look ahead as if trying to figure out where they were headed. It wasn't hard. Most of their walks ended on the bridge. Not that she minded. Actually, she wished every walk ever would end on the bridge.

She remembered the first time she had ever gone to England, before her books were published, before she'd even finished the first one. She had been working on it, though, every day. She would finish the first book during her two-week stay there. None of that mattered, though. She had been on a tour with her chorus. They had time for sightseeing, but they only walked across Tower Bridge once, at night, on their last night in London. Amelia had just finished her freshman year in high school. She was only fifteen years old.

They had just finished their last concert. They were done and reveling in it. The grueling rehearsals they had endured, six hours of singing a day, were insane, unwelcome, and unwanted by teenagers who simply wanted to experience England in all its glory. They walked across that bridge, with most of the girls mucking around in their white shirt and black skirt uniforms. Amelia joked they all looked like waitresses. None of them really bothered to take it all in. None of them except Amelia.

She had an old soul, Amelia Alverson did. She didn't realize it, but she did. You see, as all the other girls giggled, chasing each other, making plans to marry a prince, Amelia was looking at the bridge. She was taking it all in as much as physically possible, remembering every last detail. She sang one of their concert pieces, her favorite one, silently to herself, almost as a promise to herself and to the bridge that she would be back someday. One of her friends started singing one of the classic pop songs of their time. Normally, Amelia would never sing along, not in public, but looking around her, absorbing everything as if it was her last night on Earth, she gave in. She began to sing, all the while looking around her, stopping to admire all the details of the bridge that she had built out of Legos.

She would never be on the bridge, would never be in England long enough to satisfy herself. She loved it so much, felt so at home in a country that many felt isolated from. But isn't that the case with everywhere? One man's paradise is another man's prison. London, England, all of it, was her paradise.

Her little heart swelled as she continued to walk along the bridge, the bridge she felt she owned part of. It swelled as big as any heart I had ever seen swell. She was blissfully happy, and much like every other person who has ever been blissfully happy, she would spend the rest of her life looking for the same feeling. That is, until she and Joshua had started dating and walking across the bridge. It was then and only then that the bliss returned, that the feeling of being truly happy fully consumed her. It was everything she had ever wanted.

Joshua had a very important memory on that bridge—a very, very important memory indeed. It was a memory from the first time he had ever been to England with Amelia, when they had finally had a day off from shooting and she had insisted he see the bridge.

"Did you ever want to get married?" he had asked, with his hands jammed in his pocket, and his eyes fixed stubbornly on the horizon.

"Of course," she had said, "It would have to be the absolute right guy, though. The guy that every time I saw him I thought, *Wow, he's perfect.*"

"Perfect is hard to find," he had said.

"Oh, he won't really be perfect, he'll just be perfect to me. Perfect to me because I'll love him," she had replied, smiling.

Joshua smiled at that. He knew the feeling. "What

about kids?"

"I don't know. Maybe," she'd said. "What about you?"

"Yes on both counts."

"You want kids?" she'd asked, surprised, though he hadn't been sure why.

"I always have, since I was a kid myself. I want to teach my son to play ball or learn how to shoot a gun to keep guys away from my daughter while she's in ballet. I've always wanted that: a family. I had such a close family growing up, the thought of not having one is weird," he had replied.

He assumed she must have forgotten about that conversation, but he never could. He could only hope that she thought him perfect enough to marry. He would give up his perfect family if it meant waking up next to her, if that was what she wanted.

They had reached the bridge now. They walked down it slowly, taking in the view of the sun beginning to set. They ignored the people stopping dead in their tracks, surprised to see Amelia Alverson and Joshua Clemons out walking around. They were about halfway down the bridge when Joshua stopped dead in his tracks. Amelia stopped with him. They were still holding hands, after all, and she didn't want them to break apart. It didn't matter, though. He gently pulled his hand out of hers and kneeled in front of her. She looked confused, as if waiting for him to tie his shoe and then stand back up. He did nothing of the sort.

Instead, he reached into his jeans and pulled out a small red box, a box he promptly opened, a box containing a ring. A very beautiful ring at that. Joshua had enough money to buy the largest ring in the world, to have fireworks go off, to have rented out a stadium, to have done any number of things for this moment. That wouldn't have been what Amelia would have wanted, though. While she had changed Hollywood and the world, neither Hollywood nor the world had ever changed her. The ring was a small silver band with a small diamond on it, all she would have wanted. Simple, beautiful. A ring that reminded her that she would marry not for money but for love.

"Joshua—" she started to say, but he interrupted her.

"Amelia, Amelia Alverson, will you please do me the honor of becoming my wife? Will you marry your scarecrow without a brain?"

She lowered herself to her knees so that they were the same height and smiled. "And here I was thinking this was like prom and we were just going to go without bothering with the asking."

He smiled. "Is that a yes then?"

"Of course it's a yes!" she said, still smiling. He slipped the ring on her finger. It was a perfect fit.

He stood and pulled her to her feet where he promptly pulled her into a long, loving kiss, before she wrapped her arms around his neck and he pulled her to him.

"Don't give yourself such a hard time," she whispered in his ear. "You have a brain. You just still don't fully comprehend how to use it."

CHAPTER EIGHTEEN
SNOGGING

Weddings are complicated. Fun, but complicated. Weddings when you're a celebrity are even more complicated because of the number of people that would kill for any kind of information about them.

"How are we even going to tell the public about this?" Amelia asked Joshua, tucking her legs under her as he walked into the room, with water in hand, only to plop down on the sofa next to her.

"I don't know, what do people normally do? Tweet about it?"

She laughed. "Maybe?"

"We could always go on a talk show and announce it. Talk show hosts are always begging for an interview anyway," he said with a shrug, taking a swing from his glass.

The television was on, showing a replay of their latest television obsession. They may have not had much time on their hands, but that never affected their television obsessions. They loved finding new, clever shows to watch. Joshua still had a weird fetish for reality television. Amelia was trying to rid him of what she considered a bad habit by replacing it with British mysteries. He was slowly converting. They paid no attention to the television set, though. Too absorbed were they in their own conversation. It had been a week and only Lucas and Eva knew. Amelia was correct in saying that they needed to start telling people. It was always best when the media was told things and not when they simply found them out. It was bound to be a big deal. They might as well be the ones to tell it.

"I'm set to go on one for the show in two weeks but I don't really want to wait until then to tell everyone," she said, snuggling up next to him once he had put his glass down.

"Me neither," he agreed.

"How about our families?"

"Let's just call them right now."

"Don't even bother opening your mouths, I know why you've come," Lucas said, throwing open the door to his and Eva's flat.

"Um, okay?" Amelia asked.

"I suppose your outfits are acceptable. Mills, your hair looks good. Joshua, did you get a haircut?" Lucas asked, looking them over.

"Naw, he had an accident with a lawnmower," Amelia replied, grinning as Lucas ushered them inside.

"I was worried that was the case," Lucas said.

"What's wrong with my hair?" Joshua asked, offended. "I like it shorter like this."

"Nothing," Lucas said, turning around to pinch Joshua's cheek in a condescending manner.

"I still need new friends," Joshua said, frowning.

"No, you still don't," Amelia and Lucas said at the same time, high-fiving.

Amelia turned to Lucas. "What's the plan?"

"Don't tell me you have a plan," Joshua said, his shoulders slumping. "Please tell me that just this once you decided not to come up with some weird scheme."

"I can't and so I shan't," Lucas said, smiling broadly.

"We're in for it," Amelia said, giving Joshua a look. They both started to slowly back toward the door.

Lucas grabbed their shoulders and pulled them back. "Not so fast, you two. I promise this time it's a super reasonable plan."

"So we should run as fast as we can?" Joshua asked.

"Shut up, heh?" Lucas asked, narrowing his eyes for comedic effect.

"I'm guessing it involves the back yard," Amelia

said.

"Why?" Lucas asked, rolling his eyes as if he regretted asking but it had to be done like taking disgusting medicine to get rid of the flu.

"You have dirt on your hands, you're barefoot, and there are flecks of dirt on your toes."

"Reading *Sherlock Holmes* again, Mills?" Lucas asked, cleaning his wrist with his white shirt.

"Always," she replied, smiling broadly.

"My favorite detective," Lucas replied, ruffling her hair. "Now, as bloody typical, Mills is correct. My plan does indeed involve the outdoors."

Amelia wore a sleeveless black dress with flowers at the tips matched with brown sandals. Her blond hair seemed to float over her shoulders as she basked in the sunlight that London was finally getting. Joshua wore a white shirt and cargo shorts along with flip-flops. Black Ray Bans pushed back both of their hair, making them look all the more like the movie stars that they were. Lucas wore a nice white shirt and brown pants. He was barefoot, with his muddy feet treading dirt all over the house, much to Eva's dismay when she would get home.

Lucas led them out his living room to the patio where he had pushed all of his chairs and table to the side, leaving the wooden deck empty of all distractions. Looking out, they saw his muddy yard, recently watered, with its big oak tree in the middle. Lucas seemed to have recently cleaned up the yard, too, moving everything over to the side. There was a bucket of rose petals along with a camera next to the tree. What looked to be white sheets hung from the tree in celebratory fashion. Eva wouldn't like that part, either.

"Lucas Evans, what have you got planned?" Amelia asked, shaking her head, trying to hide her smile.

He shrugged and tried not to look too proud of himself. "You're movie stars. If you're going to announce your engagement, you should do it in a movie."

"You've got to be kidding me," Joshua said, shaking his head with a slight laugh.

"Do you two need makeup? Because Eva is out and that might be tricky..." Lucas said, raising his eyebrows and grinning maniacally.

"Ew no. The less stuff we put on my face, the better," Amelia said, wrinkling her nose in that way that Joshua loved.

Joshua laughed and pulled her to him, kissing her on the head. "If she's good, so am I."

"Wow, so glad I wasn't your makeup artist," Lucas said to Amelia, who beamed at him.

In the end they ended up making a sort of music video type thing. They threw rose petals at each other. Lucas guest starred popping open champagne. It was all very sweet. They released it that night and it got millions of hits. Everyone was, understandably, in love with it. It was clear how much fun the three of them had making it. They all looked delighted to be behind the camera together again, laughing, getting out water guns and shooting each other. That bit was in the blooper part of the video, throwing water balloons. It was adorable. They may have been in their late twenties, but that didn't mean that they weren't going to have fun with it. Age is but a number, after all.

"What kind of a wedding do you want?" Joshua asked, pouring Amelia lemonade as she brought the steaming plates of spaghetti Bolognese over to the table and placed one at each of their places at the table.

"I was thinking summer. Less of a chance it will rain," she said, smiling. Amelia wanted to be married in London. She was trying to find the best way to bring it up with Joshua.

"Probably right," he replied for a grin. "Never mind bad luck, everyone will be in a horrible mood if they have to bring umbrellas."

"Do you want indoors or outdoors?" she asked, sitting down across from him.

"You're the bride, you decide," he said, smiling at her as he spun the spaghetti around his fork and brought it to his mouth to blow on it gently. Steam issued from it.

"I don't want to do that, though. It's *our* wedding. We should both get to pick out aspects of it. For everything

I pick out, I want you to pick out something. I don't want to be that bride that does everything but the groom doesn't want to upset so he doesn't say anything," she replied, bringing spaghetti to her lips and popping it in her mouth.

"Well," Joshua said, smiling, "I want an indoor wedding with an outdoor reception. Of all the weddings I've been to, those are the best ones."

"Okay. I think we should have it here."

"Why?" he asked, confused.

"Because we live here. It's our new home of sorts. A lot of our friends live here now. I just think it would make sense to do it here. What is your counterargument?" she asked, slightly amused.

Joshua and Amelia had this deal that whenever they wanted to discuss something when they had different views, instead of arguing like most people would, they acted like it was a debate. They would each offer their side of the argument and whichever argument made the most sense won. It was strange, I'll admit. Lucas teased them about it quite a bit. He claimed it reminded him too much of a courtroom and that love should never be in a courtroom. What he didn't know was that I spent a lot of my time in a courtroom, in different forms, but I am almost always there. What Lucas didn't understand was that doing the debate strategy meant that Joshua and Amelia almost never fought. All decisions were final and absolutely no grudges were held.

"I don't have an opposing argument. Having it in Tennessee would have meant your family would have had to all fly out. Having it in California would mean that my family would have to fly out here. This works, this way our families get to see how we live. I like that," he said, smiling.

"Okay, where do you want to have it here?" she asked, smiling back at him.

"British Museum. We could rent out a small part of it," he said, grinning.

"Really?" she asked. She had always wanted to get married in a museum.

"We have a lot of history. It's only fair," he replied, still grinning.

She laughed. "I'll have to remember that to put it on the invitation."

"Yes, yes you will," he replied.

She leaned into his kiss, languishing in his touch behind her neck. He never went too far and made her uncomfortable, never tried to grab something he shouldn't. He was perfect, incredible at kissing, incredible at everything. He may have proposed, but he knew her limits, and he knew when not to go over them.

He touched her everywhere, with one hand on her face and his thumb tracing circles on her cheek, and his other hand tracing circles on the back of her neck. She was almost on top of him now. They had just been watching television when he had kissed her and the television had become background sound to their make-out session.

She kissed him like she had never kissed him before, like every other kiss before now had been nothing and this was the only kiss they would ever share. Their kissing grew desperate, almost, like they were worried that if either one of them bothered to come up for air then they would both die or never see each other again. Each option was really the same in the end for them, for them who couldn't live without each other.

"I love you," he whispered into her lips.

"I love you too," she whispered back. His lips tasted like strawberries, the taste left over from the fruit they had eaten for dinner.

He pulled away and murmured quietly in her ear, "Do you remember when I asked you your favorite color and then wouldn't tell you mine? I couldn't tell you mine then because it would have been embarrassing. My favorite color is dark green, like your eyes when they meet mine."

She smiled and tilted her head to catch his words with her mouth. Those green eyes he so loved completely focused on him. He smelled good, like, well like *him*. Like everything that he was, like fires in a fireplace, like the beef with broccoli they had for dinner, like blankets and warmth and everything good in the world. She really did love him and he really did love her. I did adore being in this moment with them, so intimate. They didn't go further that night, although soon they would, but they did spend an evening only thinking of each other, and in a world surrounded by technology and billions of people, it was impressive.

CHAPTER NINETEEN
WEDDINGS

Joshua and Amelia's wedding was a day to remember, to say the least. In my opinion, it was the greatest wedding I had ever been to. Maybe that was because, even though I had been to so many weddings and walked down so many aisles, I had never *wanted* to walk down an aisle more, to see two people lock eyes and feel the energy course between them.

"Don't turn around now, but she looks amazing," Lucas murmured as they both faced the pastor.

"Really?" Joshua asked in a hushed tone.

"She looks stunning. No makeup, as usual," Lucas said, smiling slightly as he winked at Amelia.

"Cold feet yet?" Lucas had asked earlier that day,

225

leaning against the door of the room where she was getting ready.

"Nope," she said, smiling up at his reflection in the mirror.

"Good," he said, grinning at her and walking into the room.

"Did you get cold feet on your wedding day?" she asked.

"Of bloody course not!" he exclaimed before looking around the room. Finding it was just the two of them there, he murmured, "Yeah, a bit. I love Eva, but it's still scary, you know? What happens next? I didn't know. The thing about marriage though, kid, is that it's the greatest thing there is. If you really love the person you marry, really love them like you love Joshua, then it's the easiest and greatest thing there is."

"Really?" she asked, turning to look up at him.

"Really," he whispered softly, kissing her gently on the head. He turned to leave the room but stopped at the door and said, "You look beautiful, Mills, just by the way."

She smiled and he left.

There was one conversation between Amelia and Joshua that I never will forget, a conversation that took place the night after Joshua had proposed. Amelia had been in her room at home, reading before bed. Joshua had walked in, wearing the boxers he slept in.

"Hey," he said, smiling as he leaned against her door frame.

She looked up from her book and smiled at him. "Can I help you?"

"You know that you always can," he replied, walking in and kissing her on the head as he plopped down next to her on the bed.

She tried not to look at the way his muscles popped and moved in his chest, his chest that was hard and soft all at the same time. She would know. She did love putting her hands there when they kissed. It almost worked, almost.

"I have a question," he said, solemnly.

"Well, ask away. I'm great with interviews," she said, shoving him playfully.

He almost cracked a smile, almost. "Yeah, but in those you are always trying to seem like nothing bothers you. I don't want to know the guarded truth, I want to know the real truth."

"Well, that got deep fast," she said, turning to him, her smile still present.

"It did," he replied.

"Well, ask away."

"Why me?" he asked.

She cocked her head. "What do you mean?"

"I mean *why me*? You could have had anybody, absolutely anybody, and don't shake your head at me like that. It's true. Gosh, Ams, you were always so scared of being with a guy and you chose me. *Why?*"

"Because you taught me to trust," she said simply.

"What?" he asked, taken aback by this answer. He wasn't sure what he been expecting, but it wasn't this.

She closed her eyes like what she was about to say, hurt to do so. "My parents were never divorced. They loved each other very much. They didn't even fight much. I trusted everyone so much, so much, Josh," she said, shaking her head as if telling her younger self not to. "But I was so young, I didn't know that a guy was mean enough to play with your heart and then smash it, smash it to where I thought I would never move on from it, that you only got one chance at love and I had mine. I loved him with every particle of my body, I lived for the sight of him, for his every word. He knew it, too. He smashed my heart, pretended to like me, took away my virtue, dragged me along, and then, at the last moment, had his sister, his sister send me a note that said that he loved me, just not enough. I never saw him again after that. A lot of people get their heart broken in a worse way, but for some reason that changed me. In a weird way, it made me who I am today."

"You're kidding," Joshua said, taken aback at the pain and rawness in her voice that he almost never heard.

She smiled wryly. "I wish I were. After that, I guess it was hard trusting a guy. I always assumed they wanted to toy with me, to pretend they liked me just for kicks, to have sex with me. I guess I was scared to death that the next guy I gave what was left of my heart to would break it, too. It took me so long to fix in the first place... I didn't think I could ever fix it again. So, I stayed away from guys, I showed no emotion towards them, one way or another. Guys didn't want to date me, anyway. Typically they want girls they can have sex with and since I was so terrified of doing that, that made me boring and not worth it. They left me alone. I was happy. Then I met you. I liked you from the beginning; you seemed like such a sweet guy, always there to make me laugh and smile. Part of me knew that you were a great guy. That didn't mean that I was comfortable giving you my heart yet. It took time, a long time, for me finally let myself like you, for me to finally decide that you probably wouldn't break my heart."

"Probably?" he asked, raising his eyebrows.

"I figured that if you did, then that really was it. I was once and for all done with guys. I would just forget the whole love thing, and move on with my life, picking up the broken shards as I went, never letting you see any of it. I'd done it before. Pain is blinding at first, but over time you learn how to control it and live with it. It's hard at first, accepting its continuing presence, but you learn, you get stronger, and some days, it, it's almost bearable."

Amelia could never forget me. I was too involved in

who she was. She couldn't forget me, no matter how hard she would try.

"It's sick though, accepting that you'll always be in pain and just deciding to live with it. Humans aren't meant to live in pain. Of course, they are meant to experience pain at one time or another, it's inevitable, but living with it full time? No one should ever have to do that," Joshua said, shaking his head.

Amelia smiled. It was a sad smile. "You would be surprised what humans can do."

"I don't want to be surprised. No one, no one, should ever just have to live with pain," he insisted.

"So, to answer your question, I picked you because in a way, you picked me. You showed me that trusting someone wasn't the worst thing you could do, you showed me that sometimes, sometimes, it's worth getting your heart broken." Amelia said, gently, her hand covering his as she met his gaze.

"I'm never going to break your heart," Joshua said, earnestly.

She kissed his cheek. "I know that. I find it a bit hard to believe at times, but I know that."

He nodded, more to himself than to her. "Good."

She prodded him with her elbow. "What about you? Why me?"

He laughed. "What kind of a question is that?"

"Um, the one you just asked me?" she suggested,

grinning.

"Well that's different. It's *you*," he said, shaking his head in disbelief.

She laughed. "What does that even mean?"

"It means that you're the only person I've ever met who can make me laugh with just a look, who can make me forget everyone and everything with one touch, who makes me smile every day of my life because you're a part of it. From the moment I met you, there was no question for me. It was always going to be you, always. There could never be any one else. No one else makes me feel the way that you do," he said, looking at her, with his eyes pleading with her to understand.

She did. She really did. She kissed him full on the mouth. His lips parted at her touch. I left them like that, absorbed in each other.

Fast forward to the day before their wedding day.

Eva was pregnant with her and Lucas's first child. Amelia had figured it out the day before when they three had gone out for drinks (lemonade, in Amelia's case).

"All right, Evs, what gives? Luc has been drinking your gin and tonic all lunch. That's very unlike you. Also, Luc keeps doting on you even more than usual. Something is definitely up," Amelia had said, narrowing her nose.

What gave was she was pregnant.

"We didn't want to spoil the wedding!"

"How on Earth could you do that? We're so happy for you! Aren't we, Josh?"

"Of course we are! That's so great! How—how—?" Joshua couldn't seem to find the words.

Amelia did for him. "How far along are you?" she asked, putting her hand over his, calming him as only her touch could.

"Only a couple weeks, not enough to show yet," Eva had replied, blushing.

"Well, listen, we couldn't be happier for you. This is the best news you could have given us," Joshua said. He meant it, too. You could tell.

The wedding was beautiful, my favorite of all time because it was the happy ending I had been rooting for all along. It wasn't really the end, but I'll get there in due time.

Amelia's dress was sleeveless, tighter at the top, loose and flowy at the bottom. She wore no train, as she found them much too long and much too annoying. Her hair was down and slightly curled for the occasion, tumbling around her face. She didn't wear heels. She would have been taller than Joshua, something she didn't want because she was worried it would embarrass him. I still don't think he would have cared either way. He wore a black tuxedo, and no product in his hair. Amelia loved to fluff it up and ruin whatever goop he had put in there.

Lucas had taken to doing it, too. He did look handsome though, with his brown eyes shimmering, and his smile contagious and *"cramping Lucas' style."* There were no cold feet for him, either. He had waited too long for this not to be sure.

"Remember the day you first met her?" Lucas said, leaning against his door frame now.

Joshua grinned. "Of course."

Lucas smiled. "You told me you were going to marry her."

"I did," Joshua affirmed.

"Good on you mate, good on you."

It was a small wedding, no more than sixty people. Amelia wanted to be able to talk to everyone for longer than a few seconds, and have no media. They picked a secluded part of the British Museum. It truly was lovely. All of their friends were there, the friends they had made acting. *Not* Jamie Hughes, but Michael was there, Michael Roberts. Patrick Green was there. Amelia saw him after the ceremony was over. She didn't need to talk to him, he had directed her for years. They had written every script together. Words were of no use to them. They knew the words of the other one all too well. He did, however, raise his glass, with a smile across his lips.

"Only you could play Claire because of this, because

if you hadn't, none of us would be here today," he seemed to say.

She smiled, a smile that seemed to be from another time. Patrick remembered the first time he had met her, headstrong and brilliant. She hadn't seemed happy though, not like now. Now she radiated happy, the kind of happy you couldn't act out for a play or a film. She was a star now, a star of his and her own making. He smiled to himself. *Whoever said blondes were dumb hadn't met Amelia Alverson.*

CHAPTER TWENTY
FIRST TIMES

They were kissing. They were married. Nothing had ever felt better or more right. Joshua hadn't been sure where he wanted this to happen, this first time where they finally took things further than kissing. He wanted it to be so perfect, so memorable. He hadn't learned. It had taken him until now, until this very second, with her lips pressed against his, her hands slowly beginning to undo the buttons on his shirt, his hands trying to figure out a way to pull hers over her head without breaking the kissing, without stopping any of it. It had taken him until now when they were back in their Tower Bridge home, when everything he had tried to make go right went wrong, to understand that it didn't matter where or when. It was only the who that mattered. Unlike the rest of it, he had the right who.

He had tried to make things romantic on their honeymoon in Italy. It had rained. He had tried to make it romantic here. More rain. He hadn't wanted rain; he had wanted perfection. He had been so disappointed, convinced that there was no way she would have him unless everything was perfect, unless the moment was perfect. He had been so sure, and yet, like she had been doing from the moment she met him, she had proved him wrong.

She was on top of him. The scent of her overwhelmed every pore of his body. She smelled like rain, like salty rain, like the outdoors, trees, grass, like lilacs, her deodorant, like everything he loved all wrapped into one. Her slim arms were on either side of his head as she held herself up, kissing his lips, his nose, occasionally biting his lip, an action which sent every fiber of his being into overdrive, a kind of primal overdrive. She knew it, too. She was close but not close enough. He wiped her hands out from underneath her and rolled until she was underneath him and he was on top of her. She laughed, an airy kind of breezy laugh into his mouth, the kind of laugh that sent chills down Joshua's spine, good kind of chills.

The kissing intensified until I was unsure who was who, their bodies moving in unison, their minds wanting the exact same thing. There was no desire to sleep there, there was only the desire to make up for the rain outside, the desire to have each other in the kind of way that only true love could produce.

She reached down and unbuttoned his jeans. Her body continued to move with his. Her other arm wrapped around his neck, anchoring her to him—as if he could or would ever let her go. He lifted his left hand off of the bed, supporting himself with his right arm, as he reached down and undid the button on her jeans. They both stood up, heaving as they pulled their pants off, throwing them on the floor carelessly. They didn't care. She leapt up against him, with her legs wrapping around his bare torso as he put her back down on the bed, crawling up over her, kissing his way up, inch by inch. She bit her tongue so no moans would come out, but they were coming out in her mind. She wanted him so badly, she didn't want to wait patiently while he sorted out the protection, she didn't want protection, she just wanted him and for once in her life, she was unprepared to wait for a result. She was as restless as a lioness about to pounce upon her prey. He didn't have to ask her how far she was willing to go. He could sense it. She was finally ready.

He wanted to take it slow. Really he did, to savor the moment, savor it all, but he just couldn't, he just couldn't wait, not anymore. He had done his fair share of waiting to get the girl, now he had her and waiting was a thing of the past. She was his and he was hers. Why not make it official in the most intimate way possible? She shivered, it was cold in the apartment, but that wasn't why. Protection sorted, he finally reached her face in his kissing journey, kissing her gently on the lips and then on the nose. The kisses were gentle, so gentle that they should have killed the passion. They would have with anyone else, except Amelia wasn't just anybody, she was the girl he was meant to be with, and the kisses in no way killed her passion. They heightened it. She grabbed his face in her hands, holding it steady, and biting her lip for a moment, trying to decide what she wanted to do now that she had his face, a movement that only turned him on more. She finally settled on kissing him right between the eyes, where he nearly went cross eyed trying to keep her completely in his sight. She pulled away, smiling. She was ready for this, whatever this would be. It wasn't a surrender, far from it. It was an agreement, an agreement to trust each other in every way, in whatever they were about to do. It was a treaty he would have cut off his right arm to sign.

She laughed softly at his face, at the expression in those warm brown eyes, at the lust that must have been reflected in her own green ones. Joshua leaned down and kissed her neck. She kissed his. Finally, kissing just wasn't enough, none of it was enough, they couldn't go too far, not these lovers, the ones who had waited so very long for this moment, knowingly and unknowingly. Lovers who had been through so much, had fought so hard to be with each other. For them, this moment was the catalyst, the fuse that would blow up the bomb, eliminating all boundaries between them, not that there had been too many before.

He pulled away for a moment to look at her. "You're beautiful."

"Shut up," she mumbled, kissing him.

He had to say it though, to get this out, to capture this moment in a time capsule to be preserved forever, never to be forgotten or thrown away. She was so beautiful to him, with her golden hair spread across the pillow, her hands now pressed against his chest, those luminescent green eyes that, despite the darkness, shone, the pupil huge and round showing the desire that was behind his every motive. How he loved her.

"No, I mean it, you really are beautiful," he said, trying to make her understand.

She smirked. "You're beautiful too, you know."

"No."

"No?"

"No. Not like you. Any guy would kill to have you," he murmured into the darkness, marveling at the woman before him.

"And yet you didn't have to kill anyone," she said softly, "Except me."

"How did I kill you?"

"With the suspense. All of this suspense is killing me."

"Well, I just might be able to do something about that."

"I was hoping you would be able to."

"I'm sorry I made you wait so long." Amelia's hand gently traced a circle on Josh's.

"You didn't make me wait too long. You made me wait just long enough to where I wanted it so bad I thought I might die, but not to the point where I actually did die."

"Are you saying I found a perfect medium?"

She laughed into his chest, a soft, musical laugh that made him fall for her all over again.

They lay in bed. Soft light streamed in through the windows, through the door covered up by drapes that led to a porch with a perfect view of Tower Bridge. The light bounced off of their faces, off of their shining eyes, of their hair, of the floor. The light almost seemed to come from them, from their smiles, from their tired muscles, from everything that they were. Amelia lay with her head on Joshua's bare chest, with his arms wrapped protectively around her. Her eyes were closed as if she were worried that opening them would ruin the moment. Joshua's eyes were wide open and glued to her. The blankets covered them.

"You sound like a teenage boy," she murmured.

He smiled. She couldn't see it but she could sense it. "I felt like a teenage boy."

"But you'd done it with other people, so it wasn't exactly your first *time*, so you weren't *that* affection starved," she said, opening one eye and grinning up at him.

"Not the same."

"Oh, please."

"No, I'm serious. It's not the same at all. You would think it would be, but it's the furthest thing from the same thing," he replied. His thumb traced circles on her arm. He could have brought up the man she lost her virtue to, how this hadn't exactly been her first time either, but he wasn't cruel, not like that.

"Sure about that?" she asked, amused at his sincerity.

"Positive," he replied.

"Well, in that case do you need to go call Luc? Tell him every detail?" she asked, trying to suppress a smile and sound serious.

"No."

"No?"

"Are you going to see him tomorrow? Is that it?"

"Maybe."

She nuzzled her nose into his chest as she laughed. The action made him feel all warm and tingly on the inside. "You two are unbelievable."

"You mean awesome?"

"Nope, I mean complete and totally *unbelievable*."

"Why?"

"Did he tell you, when he and Eva, you know," she poked his stomach.

"Maybe."

"Seriously?"

"He's my best friend," Joshua said, sounding more wounded than he actually was. She knew it, too.

"Mine too. Even so, I *highly* doubt he is going to want details," she replied.

"He might. You don't know what we talk about," Joshua pursued. He had no intention of giving Lucas details but he knew how amused Amelia would be about the whole thing.

"I've hung around you two for years. I know *exactly* what you talk about," she replied.

"Fine, what do we talk about then?" His thumb was still tracing circles on her arm. Now her thumb, which had been covering his hand, began to trace circles too, synchronizing them.

"Sports, girls, the fact that neither of you seemed to know your lines—" she began, laughing.

"Um, excuse me: we *always* knew our lines. *You* didn't know *your* lines," he replied, loving the feeling of her body shaking with laughter against his.

"I *wrote* the lines. I either knew them or I thought they were bad and rewrote them orally. Nothing out of the ordinary," she replied, laughing so hard that tears sprang to her eyes.

"Totally ordinary to have written a book series that was ready to be a movie by the time you were twenty-one," Joshua replied.

"No doubt most people do."

"I didn't."

"There always has to be one rule breaker, I guess. Unfortunately for me, I married him," she replied. Her laughter calmed down, but her smile stayed as electric as ever.

"It is very unfortunate for you," he agreed.

"I have horrible taste."

"In novels? I couldn't agree more."

"Shut up," she replied, still smiling. With her voice soft, she sounded tired, Joshua noticed.

"Did you want to get some sleep?" he asked, gently.

It was in the very early hours of the morning. Being summer, the sun rose early. They had been up all night. They were both tired but not quite ready to admit it. They wanted to sleep but they didn't want to leave each other behind, to end their conversation, even for a couple of hours. They would have loved to not require sleep and be able to spend the night talking among other things. Unfortunately, they were, after all, only human. They were limited in the amount of time they could go without sleep.

She shook her head into his chest.

"We probably should, though," he murmured. His voice began to drawl with sleep and exhaustion.

She nodded into his stomach.

"In that case, good night, Ams." He kissed her head.

"Good night, Josh." She kissed his hand.

CHAPTER TWENTY-ONE
LOVE STORY

"They've been back there forever!" Joshua exclaimed as he paced the maternity ward waiting room.

"Josh, these things take time," Amelia exclaimed, taking his hand gently in her own as he passed her chair, forcing him to stop before he wore out the carpet.

"Yeah, but stuff could go wrong. We won't know," he said. He wasn't as calm in stressful situations as Amelia.

"Eva will be *fine*," she said, firmly.

"But what if she's not? Women *die* in childbirth," Joshua informed her as if this was shocking new information.

"In the 1800s?" Amelia replied.

"So what?" he demanded, pulling his hand out of hers and resuming his pacing.

"Medicine has come a long way since then," she replied, rolling her eyes.

"Has it come far enough, though?" he asked, stopping once more to consider the question he had just asked.

"Okay, you need a distraction. Bad," Amelia said.

"What kind of distraction?" he asked, suddenly interested.

"Your turn to tell me a story." she said, smiling.

"Ams, I can't tell stories. I'm the most uncreative person ever," he said, confused as to why she would suggest such a thing when she knew his limits.

"That's why you don't have to make it up. Tell me about the first time Lucas and Eva met and how they fell in love. I've never heard that story before," she said, calmly.

"You haven't?" Joshua asked, surprised.

"Nope."

"Well..."

It had all begun a long time ago, not too long after Joshua and Lucas had met, but just long enough for them to become best friends.

Lucas had seen Eva across a crowded club, the very club where Joshua and Lucas had received their calls letting them know that they had their parts in the *Aliens* films.

"See that girl?" Lucas had asked, poking Joshua.

"Which one?" Joshua had asked, squinting through the strobe lights toward the throng of girls dancing in the center of the dance floor. It was two years before the boys would meet Amelia.

"The one with the long, wavy, brown hair in the white tank top with black jeans and heels," Lucas had said.

Joshua glared at him for a moment. That was an incredibly specific description, very unlike Lucas, before looking back to the dance floor and locating the girl. "I think so."

"I'm going to go talk to her."

"You mean hit on her?" Joshua had asked, amused. Lucas was a bit of a player. Being a good-looking wealthy actor with an accent made it easy to be so. Joshua knew this all too well, constantly having to play his wingman.

"No, I mean talk to her," Lucas had said, holding his drink tightly so that it wouldn't spill. He could have left it on the table. He *should* have left it on the table. With that, he began to make his way over to her.

There were several things about Eva that Lucas didn't know as he walked over there, the first one being that she was there with her friends because one of her friends had just been dumped, the second one being that Eva didn't give her number to guys at clubs, no matter how good-looking and foreign they were.

He tapped her on the shoulder and shouted over the

music, "I love this song, too."

She gave him a weird look. She was used to being hit on by guys at clubs. She really was a beautiful girl, and had heard just about every pickup line in the book, but somehow the handsome man in front of her seemed different. She moved away from her friends so that she could hear him and they wouldn't.

"Look, my friend just got dumped. Guys are jerks. If she sees me talking to you then she'll kill me, and frankly, I'll kill me." Eva had replied over the music.

"I'm not a jerk," he had said.

She glanced him up and down skeptically. He really was good-looking. "Then what are you?"

"An alien," he said, smiling.

"With that accent? From where? Cardiff?" she had asked, amused. Her brown eyes were dancing.

He laughed. "London."

"Well, London, it's nice to meet you," she had replied, smiling. There was something different about this guy. She thought she recognized him, though she wasn't sure from where.

"Actually, it's Lucas," he had replied.

"London, Lucas, sounds the same to me," she had said, rolling her eyes just like Amelia would one day.

"Well then you should come to London. I promise you, we look quite different," he had replied.

She grabbed his beer glass and threw it in his

face, smiling. She had always wanted to do that, but she always played the good girl in movies, not the one who threw drinks in a guy's face. Instead, she always played that girl's best friend. Maybe it was time for a change, to test the man who stood before her. "Says who?"

She thought he would be put off and leave. Instead, he didn't even bother to wipe the beer off of his face. "You when you see it."

"I just threw beer in your face and you're still on about that?"

"You're still standing here. You were supposed to walk away. So, yes, I'm still on about that," he had replied, grinning.

"You don't give up easily, do you?" she had asked, smiling.

"Nope. But you'll learn that soon enough," he said, with a wink.

She rolled her eyes again. He liked it when she did that. "Will I now?"

"You will because I'm going to need your number if we're to go to England," he replied, still smiling as the beer dripped down his face, hitting his shoes, not that he cared. Joshua was dying of laughter in the corner.

"I just don't know that I want to see you again," she said. She did, but she was playing hard to get.

"I'm quite sure you do," he said.

"And why is that?" she had asked, intrigued.

"Because I'm an excellent dancer."

"Are you now? Well, if your dancing if half as good as your ego is big, then I'm in for a treat," she had said, unable to resist a smile.

"You are in luck. My dancing is better than even my large ego can boast. Now, may I have this dance?" he asked, bowing, a feat not easily accomplished in the crowded club.

"I'm here with my friends. Remember, guys are the enemy?"

"You can throw another beer in my face."

"Make it a martini and I'm in."

"Martini it is."

They actually danced for the next hour and a half and he did get drenched in a martini. Joshua stood off to the side, smiling, and pulled out his phone to read an article on the psychology behind dating that had appeared on his social network page. Amelia was eighteen, and little did he know it, but she had seen the same article on her social network newsfeed and had read it, too. She thought it was ridiculous. He thought it was brilliant.

Lucas and Eva would go on to have an amazing night, the beginning of an amazing life. He was able to get her number and after that, there was no more messing around for him. He was done with one-night stands with other women. He only needed Eva, the strong-willed girl who threw drinks in his face.

For their first real date, they had gone ice skating in an empty, secret ice rink that Lucas knew about. He hadn't been very good at skating, not that it mattered. She wasn't, either. They spent the entire date falling over and helping each other back up, only to fall back down again. It was comical but also sweet. They would pull the other one down sometimes and stay down there for a long while as they laughed. That secret ice rink was where they shared their first kiss. It was romantic—the cold, the ice, the laughs. Joshua was very proud of his best friend, mostly because he had been trying to get him to do this sort of thing, to no avail. Only Eva could change Lucas's mind. They would go on many dates after that until it was obvious to everyone that they were dating. Rumors spread in gossip magazines. Articles popped up on websites. They ignored all of it.

They were both in acting to act, not to be famous. Being famous was a sad side effect, something unavoidable in that line of work. The constant prying bothered them, but they would work hard to figure out ways to avoid the camera, just like Amelia and Joshua did. Though they weren't nearly as big of household names as they would be after the *Aliens* films, they were still in high demand. They told each other everything. Secrets had no place of any kind in their relationship. They constantly asked the other for advice and made sure to support each other in whatever their current endeavor was.

Dating was difficult with both of their busy schedules, but they managed. They managed because the very idea of living without one another was something that simply would not do. Eventually, Eva would leave acting altogether, deciding that her preferred career had to do with creating clothing lines and setting up a charity that for each piece of clothing bought would give a piece of clothing to a child in need, but that's later on in our story.

All of this is not to say that they never fought. They did. They were by no means a perfect couple—not that there is one—but they always managed to forgive and forget because they learned earlier than most that I conquer all.

"Guys, it's a boy," Lucas said, breathless as he ran into the room where Joshua and Amelia were seated, as Joshua just finished up the story of how Lucas and Eva had met.

"Can we see him?" Joshua asked, with his voice hushed.

"Yeah, yeah of course. Eva has been asking about you two," Lucas replied. He wore the green surgeon pants and shirt with a net over his blond hair and the mask that had been over his mouth pulled down around his neck. He looked tired but happy, so very happy.

"How is she?" Amelia asked as they followed him back through the doors he had come.

"Brilliant, she's brilliant. She did so well," Lucas said, beaming from ear to ear.

Eva's room was to the left and the three best friends walked in. Eva lay in bed. The hospital bed was pushed up to a seating position. Her brown hair was damp and pulled back. Her face was covered in a thin layer of sweat. She looked exhausted, but she was beaming. Her brown eyes lit up at the sight of them. In her arms, though, in her arms was a tiny bundle, no bigger than Joshua's forearm. Joshua rushed forward and, after having given Eva a kiss on the head, took her baby from her and lifted him into his arms.

"He has Eva's hair but your eyes, Luc," he said, after a moment of studying the child.

"He's adorable," Amelia said, coming to stand behind Joshua, placing her hand on the small of his back.

"Thank you," Lucas and Eva said at the same time. Lucas had gone to sit down on the hospital bed with Eva. Her head rested on his shoulder as they watched their two best friends with their child.

"What's his name?" Amelia asked, as Joshua bounced him up and down.

"Well, we spent a lot of time thinking about this..." Eva said with a smile.

"His name is Joshua Andrew Evans."

CHAPTER TWENTY-TWO
MASTERS of DISGUISE

"Amelia, something has happened."

"Josh, what's going on? Has something happened?"

"Ams, how fast can you be at the hospital?"

"Josh, *what is happening*?"

"I can't tell you, not over the phone, just please grab a cab and get here as soon as you can."

"Josh, have you been crying?"

"Amelia, *please.*"

"I'll be there as soon as I can."

Amelia raced into the hospital. She jumped in the elevator, throwing caution to the wind. Had Joshua been hurt? No, no, because then he wouldn't have been the one to call her, so what was it then? Who was hurt?

"Ams!" Joshua exclaimed upon seeing her as the

elevator doors opened into a waiting room with chairs and a desk. His hair was wet from the snow outside. London had snow, in March. It was a miracle, and yet maybe it was also the worst thing that could have happened. Joshua hadn't even stripped off his grey coat. His jeans were slightly damp, too, as were his tan colored shoes. His jean shirt was buttoned all the way to the last button. His eyes were red. He had been crying.

She threw her arms around his neck, so relieved was she at the sight of him whole and unhurt. He kissed her ear before pulling away to look at her. She wore black skinny jeans and grey boots along with a loose white shirt. He was relieved to see her, too.

"Josh, what happened? Is someone hurt?" she asked. Her eyes searched his face.

"Ams, it's Lucas and Eva."

"Oh my gosh."

"Ams, the paparazzi were following them and they stopped for a red light and the paps just plowed right into them. Ams, they're all three in the hospital in critical condition," Joshua said all in one breath.

"No," she muttered in disbelief. The floor seemed to fall out from underneath her.

"They won't let me back to see them." His voice shook.

"They're about to," she said, walking determinedly over to the nurse's desk. "Excuse me, I don't... I don't feel well." She placed her hand over her forehead pretending as if she felt very ill. She was a very good actress for a reason. "I think... I think... I think I need to lie down."

The nurse looked alarmed. Upon recognizing her, she raced around the desk and grabbed Amelia, supporting her back as Amelia made as if to stumble.

"You need to lie down right now, miss," she said, taking her back towards the beds down the corridor where Lucas, Eva, and little Joshua would be.

Joshua picked up on what she was doing and ran over, helping to support her other side, knowing full well that she didn't need support.

"Who are you?" the nurse demanded.

"Her husband?" he suggested. Recognition flashed across her face.

"You'd better come, too." She led them behind the wooden doors and into a room where she helped Amelia lie down. "You should stay here for a few minutes, miss."

"Thank you so much. I'll come out as soon as I'm feeling better. I simply don't know what came over me, I just felt as if I was going to pass out," Amelia said with a faint voice. I smiled. She really was clever, this one.

"I'll be back to check on you in fifteen minutes," the nurse said, nodding steadily as she backed out the door. She had other problems to deal with, as did they.

The minute she was gone, Joshua pulled Amelia up, much to her annoyance, and they both glanced out the window, checking that the coast was clear.

"Lucas is in Room 223, I heard one of the nurses say," Joshua murmured.

Amelia looked down at their clothes. "They'll never let us in like this."

"Any better ideas?" Joshua asked.

Yes. There was a closet in the room that they soon discovered was home to nurses' garb. After a few minutes of trying some on, they located some that fit and pulled them on.

"We better put on the white masks. We'll be recognized otherwise," Amelia said, pulling two out and tossing Joshua one.

"I feel like we're Lewis and Claire going on another intergalactic adventure," Joshua murmured with a laugh.

"How do you think I knew that would work? It's what Claire would have done," Amelia said with a laugh.

Joshua shook his head. "No, it's what *you* would have done, so Claire would have done it."

With that, they opened the door to the hall and walked out purposefully to Room 223. The hallway was bustling with nurses and doctors all running about, trying to save people's lives. Amelia and Joshua strode toward the door, pretending that this was a movie and proceeding like they thought their characters would proceed. They encountered no objections; no one stopped them, not one person. They didn't have to go far to find Lucas's room with its wooden door. They walked in. It was a small room with a bed and two nurses bustling about, cleaning things.

They froze when they looked at the bed. Lucas's face was bloody, with a bandage covering the left side of it. His leg was hanging from the ceiling in a cast, his arm was bandaged up, and his eyes were closed. Amelia prodded Joshua and they both moved toward the bed.

"Are you here to relieve us?" one of the nurses asked. They seemed to be done with Lucas anyway, only watching him. He was a well-known celebrity, after all.

"Yes," Amelia replied in her best English accent, which incidentally was spot on.

"Brilliant," the nurse said, and the three of them left.

Amelia and Joshua moved toward the bed, pulling their masks down. "Luky-Luc, it's us, it's Amelia and Joshua. Do you recognize us?"

Lucas's eyes fluttered open and he smiled upon seeing his friends. "Do I even want to know how you two got in here?"

"Probably not yet," Amelia said softly.

"How are Eva and little Joshua Andrew?" Lucas asked. He was weak, but seeing his friends seemed to have a rejuvenating effect on him as friends so often do.

"The nurse at the front desk said that they're going to pull through," Joshua said.

Lucas nodded. "Good. That's good. The paps just

came out of nowhere. They had been following us and they must have guessed we were going home. They saw us and must have missed that there was a red light for them and just came right into us. The good thing was we were driving a black Aston Martin and they were driving a Prius. They hit my side, too. Eva and J. A. were on the other side."

"The paps are in surgery right now," Joshua said, quietly.

Lucas seemed to not have heard him. "Did I ever mention how much I hate Priuses?"

"Every day we were in L.A.," Amelia said, smiling.

"The whole time I saw them coming towards us, all I could think was that I was going to die at the hands of a *Prius* driver. That in and of itself nearly killed me," Lucas said, closing his eyes but smiling slightly.

"Stay with us," Joshua said, alarmed.

"I'm *not* staying with you lot. I have my own house— oh, you mean stay alive. I can't really die, you git. I still haven't met your child." He opened one eye and grinned. "How can I die peacefully not having a thing like that?"

"Luc, Ams isn't pregnant," Joshua said, confused.

"Yeah, no I *know* and that's the problem. When she *does* though I will need to meet your child. I wonder if it will be a boy or a girl."

"Luc, that's a long way off," Amelia said gently.

It was a boy.

CHAPTER TWENTY-THREE
ACCIDENTS

Amelia Alverson was horrible at being injured. Actually, she was horrible at being sick. Actually, she was horrible at needing help. She took every chance she had at independence. She did whatever she wanted, whenever she wanted. Much to Joshua's certain dismay when he would hear of it, she had broken her left leg on a skiing trip.

She reveled in doing things that she was told were impossible with only one leg. She loved proving people wrong, and had her whole life. Now was no different.

It was eight months later. Amelia was back in London.

"You can't go anywhere, Ms. Clemons. You are on

bed rest."

"Why?"

"Because you could seriously injure yourself and you refuse to be in the hospital."

"Why?"

"Because you are in very precarious health. Already you have hurt your leg and now you seem to be in danger of hurting everything else because of your stubbornness."

"No, I'm not. I'll be fine."

"If you think you'll be fine, if you continue going on as you do, then you seriously misunderstand the seriousness of the situation. Your leg needs time to heal back properly, lest it heal back wrong and you have problems later in life. You are misjudging your own abilities," the doctor said.

"I don't think I am."

"If you have anyone to take care of you, a friend, a boyfriend, a husband, then you should call him," the doctor advised sternly.

"My husband is just at work. He'll be home tonight."

"Good."

Joshua Clemons wasn't at work. He was getting ready to do an interview for the *Today Show* in New York City, six and a half hours by plane away from Amelia, when he got the call.

"She said you were at work," the doctor said.

"I'm on a promotional tour for my new film in the

U.S. She didn't even call me."

"It's not my place to tell you what to do, then. Go where you are needed most. Maybe she thinks she doesn't need you."

Joshua knew better. If she wasn't calling him then it was because she didn't want to disturb him. He understood that it was only a broken leg, but he also understood that, on her own, that might be a bit difficult to handle.

"What was that all about?" Lucas asked, glancing over at Joshua's pale face.

"That was the doctor. Amy is injured. She had apparently broken her leg two days ago skiing, got it patched up, and is back at home now."

"She was being Amy, basically?" Lucas asked.

"Yeah."

"Is she okay?"

"She's on bed rest, and the doctor won't let her go anywhere because she needs to let her leg heal a little first. It was apparently a very serious break," Joshua said, quietly. He should be mad. He should be furious that she had put herself in that kind of danger, but he wasn't. All he was was relived, and he knew that he would not have to talk her out of ski trips again. This had been her first in a decade and probably her last in a lifetime.

"I can call Eva and ask her to take care of her." They weren't due back in London for the premiere for another week and a half.

"I have a better idea."

Amelia lay in bed with the channel ready to watch Joshua do his interview when she heard the front door open downstairs. She was at their house on Baker Street. It was twelve hours later. Even though she had led the doctor to believe otherwise, she was more than willing to lie in bed. Well, not exactly willing, but she knew she had to. She was rebellious, but only to a point.

Quite honestly, she was also okay with the whole bed rest thing because she was in a lot of pain. The doctor had given her some medication, but she'd never broken anything before. The sensation was completely new. She had been lucky to only break one leg with the horrific fall she had experienced. She was used to pain, though, the dull throbbing sensation that took over your body and your mind. She was accustomed to being in its constant reach. This was nothing new; her childhood had taught her that.

Glancing over at the empty side of the bed next to her, she wished for the millionth time that Joshua was there. He had been gone a week, a whole week that felt like a year. Sure, she had things to do, friends to meet up with, lots to keep her busy, but none of it mattered because she hated looking at the empty bed next to her and feeling alone. He hadn't wanted to go on the tour. Tours were so tedious, so much work, so little rest, so little time to talk to Amelia. Sometimes she could come, sometimes she couldn't. He had looked for every way out of it that he could, but to no avail. In the end he had been forced to go, and she was forced to stay at home because her mother's birthday had been that weekend and she was not allowed to miss the celebration. Of course the celebration resulted in a broken leg but there was no way our Hollywood friends could have predicted that.

She couldn't think why the front door would have opened.

"Hello?" she asked, "I suggest whoever you are that you leave because I have a gun and I'm not afraid to use it!"

She heard a footfall on the stairs.

"I'm serious!" she shouted, sitting up. She was worried. She wouldn't be able to do much with one leg in a cast, propped up.

"Someone order pizza?" The door opened. It was Joshua.

Her pulse slowed and then sped up. "Josh?"

He dropped his bag on the floor and ran to her. She threw her arms around his neck as he sat down beside her. "Josh, what are you doing here? You're supposed to be on the *Today Show* in five minutes!"

"I told them that something way more important just came up: my wife," he said, smiling as he pulled away to look at her. "The doctor called. Why didn't you tell me that you needed me here?"

"Because I didn't want you to have to drop everything to come help me. I didn't want to be a damsel in distress and interrupt you because I needed you here, and *need* is a very strong word, but I follow your train of thought. If I called you every time I wanted you here, then you never would have left," she said, with her eyes roaming his face, taking him in, his smell, his everything.

"Ams, I don't want someone else taking care of you, and I certainly don't want you to have to take care of yourself. It's my job to take care of you. My second job is acting. You always come first, you should know that."

She kissed him. "I just didn't want to slow you down."

"Ams, you'll *never* slow me down. Being with you, that's when everything speeds up, because there are never enough minutes in a day to spend with you and they just seem to go by so fast," he said, with his thumb tracing her cheek.

"I missed you."

"Sorry folks, it seems Joshua Clemons can't come tonight. He had a family emergency. My guess is that it something to do with his wife, Amelia. So, instead, Lucas Evans will be talking about his and Joshua's new film."

"Hello America, hello Joshua and Mills, hope you two are having fun in London without me. And Joshua, you take care of her, mate. Now, what's your first question about the film?"

Joshua and Amelia laughed.

CHAPTER TWENTY-FOUR
WORRIES

Lots had happened in the last year: Amelia had finished her run on her British television show. She had done a movie and Joshua had done a movie. Lucas and Eva had purchased the house next door to Amelia and Joshua on Baker Street where they now lived with their son. Lucas had taken the year off from movies but would soon do another one—they needed income, after all. Eva was working on her fashion line from their house, running everything off of a computer.

Joshua and Amelia weren't working on starting a family yet. Joshua said that they should absolutely wait, that they were young and they would have plenty of time for that later. Amelia was fine with waiting. Our favorite actors had changed a lot since we first met them. They were now all grown up. Their friendship had been tested and proven true. It was about to be tested again.

"Eva," Amelia said as Eva opened the door to her house, admitting her best friend.

"What's wrong? You sounded frantic on the phone," Eva asked, leading her into the living room, little Joshua was asleep in his room.

"Is Luc home?" Amelia asked, not ignoring the question, just putting it off for the moment.

"No, just little Joshua and I. Amelia, what has happened? Are you and Joshua okay? Did something happen between you two?" Eva asked, worriedly.

Amelia shook her head. "Evs, I'm late."

"What?" Eva asked, confused by this answer.

"Evs, I'm *late*. I'm two weeks *late*," she said slowly, hoping her friend would understand.

Understanding shimmered in Eva's eyes. "Oh."

"Yeah."

"Does Joshua know?" Eva asked, not quite sure why her friend seemed so upset.

"No, please don't tell him. I'm not sure if it's anything," Amelia said.

"But it could be something," Eva correctly pointed out.

"I know, I know. I've made an appointment with a doctor who specializes in this sort of thing," Amelia said, nodding vigorously.

"Amy, you're a celebrity, you can't go walking into one of those places! Not unless you want Joshua to hear from a magazine and not from you," Eva said.

Amelia paled, "I didn't even think of that. I'll cancel right away."

"Why don't you just take a pregnancy test?" Eva asked.

"Because I want to be beyond positive," Amelia replied.

Eva paled. "Is the child not Joshua's?"

"What? No!" Amelia exclaimed. It was her turn to look confused now.

"Then what is the problem? You're married, happily. You have a home. You have enough money. Why would it be so bad to have a child right now?" Eva asked.

Amelia took a deep breath. "Because Josh is about to leave for nine months to go do a movie."

"Well, he needs to get his act in gear and pull out of the film," Lucas said firmly. He and Eva sat on the sofa. She had recounted her conversation with Amelia to him.

"But what if he can't?" Eva asked.

"Then he better figure out a way, even if it means breaking his own arm so that he is unable to do it. He can't leave her alone, not like this. He does that and we will officially no longer be best friends," Lucas replied.

"She doesn't want to get in the way of his career,

though."

"That's ridiculous. In Joshua's mind, everything gets in the way of her," Lucas replied.

"I know."

"So what is she planning on doing? He leaves in a week. Is she just going to let him leave and not tell him and then when he comes back, surprise him with a child? That's preposterous," Lucas said.

"That's what I said," Eva replied.

"So she thought of it. Listen, if she doesn't tell him, I will. I know that I'm probably not supposed to know, but he's the father. He has to know somehow. Joshua has always wanted children. He may say he doesn't want any right at this moment, but that doesn't mean he doesn't want one at all."

"Well, let's see what her test results are first before we attempt to convince her of that."

"I just talked to Joshua," Amelia said into the phone.

"You did?" Eva asked, whacking Lucas hard so that he knew what was happening. The two had been sitting on the sofa watching television when the phone had rung.

"Yeah."

"How did he take it?"

"He's really pleased."

"Is he now?" More whacking. Lucas gave Eva a look

but was too eager to overhear anything that he could of the conversation to scoot out of range.

"Yeah, did you guys want to come over for dinner tomorrow night and act really surprised? I think we both know that there was no way you didn't already tell Luc," Amelia said with a smile.

"I have no idea what you are talking about."

"Hey Luc."

"Hey Mills! Dammit. I heard nothing, I know nothing."

"Yeah, you guys are idiots and we're going to be having lasagna. See you tomorrow."

"I think my cover is blown."

"Yeah, I think Amelia might have guessed your presence."

"I swear, she's secretly Sherlock Holmes. I mean, she lives on *Baker Street*, she has an *assistant*, she owns a *trench* coat, and she loves to solve puzzles. Look at the facts."

"Luc, I think Joshua would be genuinely offended that you think of him as Amelia's assistant."

"Yeah, but, am I wrong?"

"Shut up."

273

CHAPTER TWENTY-FIVE
BABY BUMP WATCH

Telling the Internet about the child proved tricky.

"We could always do a video again."

"We did that last time. We should do something a little cleverer this time around," Joshua said firmly.

"Okay... like what?" Amelia asked. She was curled up against Joshua for a night in as they watched television. It was only a week later.

"We could send out a cute picture."

"Like just what kind of cute picture?" Amelia asked, turning her head so that she could see his face.

He kissed her nose. "We could just wait for an ultrasound and send that out."

"Isn't that a bit weird?" she asked, uncertain. "I mean, the picture could be of anything."

"It really couldn't, but I see your point," Joshua said with a nod. "How about we take our picture with the picture?"

"Still weird. Actually, the whole thing, having to announce it publicly to people that we don't know, is weird," Amelia said after a moment.

"As weird as that one time Lucas decided he would put on a fake mustache and walk around Hollywood doing errands hoping the paps wouldn't know it was him because of a fake mustache?" Joshua asked. His body shook with laughter at the memory. He and Amelia had made sure to get lots of pictures.

"Maybe that was worse," she acknowledged, laughing.

"What *was* undoubtedly worse was that he thought it looked good," Joshua said, with tears coming to his eyes at the very thought.

"You know, as his friends, we should have told him it did," Amelia said. They had immediately told him how he really looked and shaken all idea of growing a mustache from his mind.

"You're right. It would have been so much more fun."

"For us, not for him."

"We could have shown little Joshua!"

"Aw, the poor kid would have been so embarrassed he would have had no choice *but* to run away from home."

"To our house."

"Because we will be super cool parents who don't grow weird mustaches."

"Couldn't have said it better myself."

All was well, except Joshua, like the concerned husband that he was, decided that he needed to go see the doctor to make sure that he knew as much about this as he possibly could. He had cancelled his movie and stayed in London. Now he needed to make sure that he did everything he could there.

"Are there any risks?" he asked, pulling out a notepad.

Dr. Echols was the best pregnancy doctor from Los Angeles. Therefore, it made perfect sense that he would go to her. She had black hair, blue eyes, and pale skin.

"Besides the usual?" the doctor asked with a smile. She had read about Joshua and once she had heard about Amelia had been wondering how long it would be before he came to pay her a visit.

"There's a usual?" Joshua asked, alarmed.

"Joshua, she'll be fine."

"Are you absolutely sure?"

"No."

Joshua took a deep breath. "Well, I should be worried then."

"It's Amelia. She's very clever and she won't do

anything stupid to jeopardize her health," Dr. Echols said.

"That's my point. It's Amy, and she'll do something to jeopardize her heath and then be clever enough to cover it up."

"I mean, you could have just asked me about it," Amelia said over dinner that night. She wore a soccer jersey and white shorts. It was soccer night. He wore nice pants and a nice white shirt.

"I didn't think you would answer my questions honestly."

"I'm super honest!" Amelia exclaimed in mock hurt.

"You mean you're super good at leaving out the concerning part of the truth but technically telling the truth?" Joshua asked with a slight smile.

"Some things are better left unsaid."

"Look, I thought going to a specialist to ask questions was a good idea. I still think it was, even if she scared me a little," Joshua said.

"Sweetie, this is why the Internet was invented— for your weird embarrassing questions."

"Not for creepy grown men to look at porn in their mother's basement?" Joshua asked, a smile creeping across his face.

"Do you have something else that you need to talk about?" Amelia asked with a grin.

"Absolutely not."

"Good, I don't think we should have *that* conversation just yet."

"It was a joke!"

"Sure it was."

279

CHAPTER TWENTY-SIX
NEW LIFE

"What's this about you getting offered a role on Broadway?" Amelia asked, walking into the living room with a bowl of grapes for them to share as they watched Lucas appear on a British talk show.

"Nothing. I'm going to turn it down," Joshua replied with a shrug.

"Why?" Amelia asked, sitting next to him.

"Because you're here and there is no way in hell I am leaving you and going across an ocean just for some part," Joshua replied, ignoring the food and pulling her to him. "How did you even find out about that?"

"Luc told me. He also said that the role was your all-time favorite character from your all-time favorite play," she accused.

"He's such a gossip."

"Is it true, though?"

He took a deep breath but his body almost seemed to shrink with a lack of oxygen, like he wasn't breathing air. "Yeah, it's true. They just want me to sort of guest star for four months while they look for a new lead. They haven't found the perfect one yet."

"Then you have to go."

"I don't *have* to do anything. Look, there'll be other parts, other times," he replied.

"There'll be other times to watch me like a hawk, too," she said gently.

He looked at her—those green eyes, the lock of blond hair that had fallen out of her bun. "Not nearly enough."

"Look, I don't want you to leave, I never do. Every second without you is like trying to breath underwater, but I don't want to hold you back. I don't want to be the reason that you don't take a part that you really want," she said after a moment.

"You'll never hold me back. I'm not leaving you here alone, not while you're pregnant with our child. I mean what kind of a self-centered jerk do you think I am? I would sooner cut off my right arm than leave you," he replied passionately.

"Are they offering you housing?"

"What?"

"Will the production pay for your housing?"

"Um, I guess so? Why does it matter? I'm not taking the part."

"It matters because I've always wanted to live in New York and getting paid to live there for free? That sounds like a pretty sweet deal," she replied, smiling.

"Wait, so... You would come with me? Can you do that? Will you be able to travel?" he asked, elated and worried at the same time.

"Josh, I'm a month along, I'll be five months along by the time we come home, largely the right time to travel. I wanted you to go, leaving me here while you were there was never an option. You seriously think I would let you loose near a bunch of beautiful rich women unsupervised?" she asked, smiling.

"No one supervises me when I talk to you," he said, smiling back.

"That was so cheesy I'm beginning to think someone should," she replied with a laugh.

"Hey guys!" Amelia exclaimed as the screen of her phone lit up and Lucas and Eva appeared on the screen.

"Excellent, the technology actually managed to work for once," Lucas remarked with a grin.

"Luc, it worked last week when we did this..." Amelia said with a laugh.

"Yeah, but it didn't work that one time so I'll always be surprised from now on when it works," Lucas replied, with his grin growing wider.

"You're an idiot," Amelia said affectionately as she rolled her eyes.

Amelia and Joshua sat on the floor, leaned up against the glass pane door leading out to the porch of the apartment. They were fifty floors up and the New York skyline covered in snow lay behind them, ever growing as more snowflakes continued to drop from the sky. Inside the apartment was warm, though. Lucas and Eva could hear the crackling of the fireplace in the background. The beautiful, decorated, glistening Christmas tree shone its lights, reflecting off the pane behind them. Amelia wore a dark blue sweater while Joshua wore a black one. That was all that could be seen from the video screen.

"You two don't look like Christmas is today in the least!" Lucas exclaimed.

"Well that's because it's tomorrow for us," Joshua pointed out.

Lucas rolled his eyes. "Time differences are my kryptonite, you know that."

Lucas and Eva wore their Christmas morning pajamas, red ones with stripes. Eva had picked them out and while Lucas had complained at least once an hour about having to wear them, he secretly liked them. They were very soft and fluffy. The two sat on their sofa in their living room, with the Christmas tree and sounds of a pleased little Joshua in the background. He had just

284

finished opening his presents and now it was time for the adults to open theirs.

"How is New York?" Eva asked. "I've always wanted to be in New York at Christmas time!" They had wanted to come to spend Christmas with the Clemons in New York, but with little Joshua being barely two years old, they had been worried about how he would hold up on the flight. Eva didn't really celebrate Christmas either, being Jewish, but they had celebrated Hanukkah with her parents who had flown in for the season.

"Freezing," Amelia said with a laugh.

"You jest," Lucas replied.

"It's so beautiful, though. We went and saw the Nutcracker last night and then walked home and the snow was falling and it was just amazing," Joshua said.

"Excuse me while I go puke," Lucas said, but he was smiling.

"How is England?" Amelia asked.

"You will be beyond shocked to learn that it is raining," Lucas said, pulling a straight face.

"No way."

"No one is more taken aback then I, I can assure you."

"Has MI6 been notified of this shocking development?"

"I emailed them this morning. They're sending James out later today to investigate," Lucas replied,

285

referring to James Bond.

"Well, at least we've left England in good hands," Amelia said.

"Of that you can rest assured," Eva said with a laugh as she looked fondly at Lucas.

"But do you two like New York?" Lucas asked. He was slightly—not super—worried, mind you, but ever so slightly worried that his two best friends might like New York and stay.

"I mean, it's nice."

"It's super cold."

"Ams, London is cold too."

"But they have accents to make up for it."

"New Yorkers have accents, too."

"Dear God, Joshua Reynolds Clemons—" Lucas began.

"My middle name isn't Reynolds..."

"—New York has changed you."

"I think that was a factual statement... New Yorkers do have accents..."

"We'll be home before you know it, Luc," Amelia said with a smile.

"Good. If Amelia Alverson leaves England too long, it just might fall."

"Be sure to catch it," Amelia said with a grin.

"I forgot how punny you were," Lucas said with an affectionate roll of his eyes.

"How dare you."

"Apologies."

"Can I please open my presents now?" Lucas asked. "Mills sent these two months ago so that I've had to look at them every single day when I walk in the door and not open them."

"That was the plan."

"Your plan was hurtful."

"I'm not at all sorry."

"I know."

"Yeah, go ahead," Joshua said with a smile.

I looked out the window at the snow as it fell, blanketing the entire city. I looked out at the people walking along the streets, with the darkness of night slowly enveloping them. It had grown dark outside, but the room I was in was brightly lit. It shone brightly in the sky, causing the people below to look up at it, to see its light against the dark. I was in the heart of it all, surrounded by it, and Amelia and Joshua didn't even notice.

CHAPTER TWENTY-SEVEN
LUCAS PATRICK CLEMONS

The Lauren Clyde Show, 2033

"What's it like being a dad, Joshua? I heard that you rather like this dad stuff."

"It's amazing, it's the best thing there is, really. Amy and I have a little son and he's just the cutest thing in the world."

"How old is he?"

"He'll be a year old next week, so yeah. Time really does fly, I guess."

"Who does look like?"

"He has Amy's green eyes with the same intelligent look in them, even at his age, and my dark hair and my face shape. He has sort of olive skin, though. We're not sure where he got that."

"You like it, then?"

"Being a dad? I can't think of anything better. We're thinking about maybe giving him a brother or sister. We're not sure, though. He's not a difficult child at least, laughs a lot, already crawling. He's going to be an active little one, we think."

"Well, that's amazing. I think we have some pictures..."

There was a collective "Aw" from the audience.

Joshua laughed. "Thank you! His mother and I think so, too!"

Lucas, Eva, and little Joshua were all at the hospital to welcome Joshua and Amelia's son into the world.

"Guys, would you like to come back to see my son?" Joshua asked, running into the waiting room. Lucas stood, putting his weight on the cane he would have to carry around for the next month. Eva and their son rose with him.

"We thought you'd never ask."

They walked into the room. Amelia's hair was damp, but her face was dry thanks to a towel she had used to dry it. Her lips were ruby red from the exertion she had just been through, with her cheeks pink and her eyes an even brighter shade of green. She grinned at her guests and held up the little blue bundle that she had in her arms.

"Lucas Patrick Clemons, meet your Uncle Luc."

Tears sprang to Eva's eyes and she ran to embrace her best friend. Lucas stood back, though, watching his son climb up on the bed to get a good look at the boy who would one day be his best friend.

"I still can't believe that you did it," he said quietly, shaking his head.

"I know," Joshua said, smiling.

"The four of us, mate, we've been through it all. I'm surprised we haven't all died by now to be perfectly honest."

"Me too."

"We made it though. We're alive. And you know what? I think we're all alive, all still friends, because of this stuff right here. We're here for all of it: the good, the bad, and the otherwise. We've all made some mistakes, but maybe those mistakes are what brought us here. I mean, look at Mills. She didn't want a boyfriend for the longest time, thought guys would never like her, and now she's married to the guy who was in love with her for years and has a child. And look at you. You ran after a girl forever until she finally stopped running. It took guts and a lot of pain to wait that long, but you knew that you were doing the right thing and you were. Now you've married her and she loves you just as much as you love her. And then there's me. I thought I would never settle down, that

I would just act forever and ever, and that little rascal climbing on the bed is mine, as is the beautiful woman next to him. And Eva, she didn't want a boyfriend and she got a husband out of it. I'm not really sure how we all got here, mate. I just know that I'm glad that we did."

"Josh, he's opening his eyes! Come see!" Amelia exclaimed.

Joshua grinned at Lucas and together they both walked over. Her husband kissed her on the head until she caught his lips. They kissed for a long moment before both pulling away and looking down at the thing that they had made and laughing as the baby made a grab at Joshua's finger. I left the six of them like this, smiling, laughing, together.

Amelia looked up at Joshua and smiled. "We only ruled the world for a short period of time, but looking back, maybe that was all the time we needed."

EPILOGUE

So this is the end, the end of an era. If you're reading this, then you now know the true story of Amelia Alverson and Joshua Clemons. You know their friends and you know what really happened, not what it says on a grocery store newsstand. You met Lucas Evans, a legend in the cinema, and Eva Noble, a legend in the fashion industry.

What happened to all of them? You need only watch the late night biography channels to find out. They're almost always running something about one of the four of them and their children. Jamie Hughes went on to become a director, one day calling Amelia and asking her to do a part in one of his films since he felt no one could do it but her. She would win an Oscar for it. Michael Roberts would go on to marry his best friend from his childhood. Amelia and the others would all attend the wedding. Patrick Green passed away a decade after Amelia and Joshua's wedding of lung cancer. Eva and Lucas would go on to have three more children, two more boys before finally having a little girl. Boys had a hard time asking that beauty on a date thanks to her three overprotective brothers. Joshua and Amelia would continue to do movies and be in plays and Amelia would write many more bestselling novels, so long as nothing interfered with picking their children up from school. They would have three. Two boys and a girl who would have the same problem as her best friend: Amelia Evans. Joshua and Amelia were happily married for the rest of their lives, never regretting having chosen each other.

This all happened a very long time ago, of course. Their marriage was in 2030, no doubt before you were born, so wherever you've found this novel, in an old chest, or on a bookshelf where you never noticed it before, know that it chose you. Great love stories are only great because people know about them, or at least that is the common belief. If you have this book, then there is no reason for you to tell anyone about it. You know the truth, as I said before: Amelia and Joshua never cared about people knowing the truth.

So, if you are reading this then I offer you this final piece of advice: I am everywhere and everything. You may not see me for a very long time, or you may see me tomorrow. I have no way of knowing. My advice is this: I'm coming eventually, so never lose faith. Sometimes all you need to do is wait. Of course, sometimes you will find me.

Naturally, this is all a true story.

There is something that Amelia wrote in her autobiography years after all this happened, toward the end of her life, that truly struck me. I think I will leave it here for you, dear reader.

"When I was younger, I was convinced that for someone to love you, you had to be perfect, flawless. I thought that you could never achieve love unless you were that, that love was a sort of prize after all the hardships you endured to get there. That wasn't true, though, not in the least. I wish I could go back in time and tell myself what I know now, but I can't so I will tell you. The point of love isn't to be perfect to achieve it; the point of it is to find someone who loves you because you *aren't* perfect. Love isn't going to solve all of your problems. Sometimes it might even create more. But if it's the real thing, like what I found, then the point of love is to give you someone to face the problems with, to not push away or hide but to let in. Maybe that's the point of youth, to figure that out, to find the truth of love for yourself so that when you find the real thing you know just how lucky you are. Find your searchlight and follow the beam. Sometimes the light will hurt, but the warmth of what you will find is irreplaceable. Maybe I needed to feel the burn before I could see the light.

Epilogue

I sent out my searchlight and let it bring me back to life and that is all that is perfect about me."

296

ACKNOWLEDGMENTS

The author would like to acknowledge:

Ann Jacobus – Thank you for all of your patience, your guidance, your gentle pushes, and all of your encouragement. This book would not be the book that it is if not for you.

Naomi Kinsman – Thank you for choosing to support a teenager who had a story to tell and for patiently helping me tell it.

To my parents – Thank you for your never-ending encouragement and love. Your support never wavered, even when, I'm sure, the story in my head was tough to see in yours.

Flo – Thank you for being the best friend anyone could ever ask for. Your enthusiasm and passion for my books never fails to make me smile. I hope you like it and have lots of ships to Argo!

Tris – Thank you. Just thank you. For all the edits, all the phone calls, all the harsh reality checks. You've seen this book through from beginning to end and I can't thank you enough for it. Words cannot express how thankful I am that you never fail to let me bounce an idea off of you, read you a scene, or talk about a character for an hour because I need to hear myself talk out loud to work through everything and occasionally needed an answer. Thank you.

Ansley – Meuf! Thank you for your support of this novel, of me, of the ships, canon and not so canon. You've been here from the beginning of this book and now you are at its end. This all started because you dared me to do it, to see if I could really write a romance novel. I guess I'm more successful with completing dares than we both thought. Challenge accepted. This was Legend—wait for it—Dary, LEGENDARY.

Lauren – Thank you for all of your help throughout this

whole process. I love that I can just come to you and talk about a problem that I'm having without needing to explain myself. You just get it, and you always offer the best advice. Our history chats are part of what has shaped this novel and will hopefully continue to shape further ones. Long may our friendship reign.

Conor – Thank you for being the best brother in the whole world, for letting me rant and think and rant some more. You the real MVP.

Carter – Thank you for giving this a try when I know that it wasn't exactly what you are used to.

Clemie – Thank you for always being there and for giving your advice when you could.

Leo – Thank you for all of your praise and constant support and for always being there for me. I don't know that I'm as clever as you seem to think I am, but I'll do my best to try. The sarcasm will always be real but you still have one of the best personalities in the universe. Cheers.

Ishan – Thank you for your theater expertise. Joshua would never have done theater if you hadn't showed me just how amazing it is.

Alesha – Thank you for all of your support and all of your help. Your enthusiasm never wavers.

Nicole – Thank you for your aid in developing these characters.

And to this reader for reading all the way through the acknowledgements – Thank you for giving a new author a try and for getting to know Amelia, Joshua, Lucas, and Eva along with me. This book never would have been possible if it weren't for you.

CPSIA information can be obtained
at www.ICGtesting.com
Printed in the USA
BVHW061028020519
547198BV00017B/1170/P